THE SELECTION STORIES

THE PRINCE
& THE GUARD

ALSO BY KIERA CASS

The Selection
The Elite
The One

THE SELECTION STORIES

THE PRINCE & THE GUARD

KIERA CASS

An Imprint of HarperCollinsPublishers

HarperTeen is an imprint of HarperCollins Publishers.

The Selection Stories: The Prince and The Guard
Copyright © 2014 by Kiera Cass

Library of Congress catalog card number: 2013953798
ISBN 978-0-06-231832-9 (pbk.)

Typography by Sarah Hoy
13 14 15 16 17   CG/RRDH   10 9 8 7 6 5 4 3 2 1

First Edition

CONTENTS

THE PRINCE

CHAPTER 1

I PACED THE FLOOR, TRYING to walk the anxiety out of my body. When the Selection was something in the distance— a possibility for my future—it sounded thrilling. But now? Well, I wasn't so sure.

The census had been compiled, the figures checked multiple times. The palace staff was being reallocated, wardrobe preparations were being made, and rooms were being readied for our new guests. The momentum was building, exciting and terrifying in one fell swoop.

For the girls, the process started once they filled out the forms—thousands must have done so by this point. For me, it started tonight.

I was nineteen. Now, *I* was eligible.

Stopping in front of my mirror, I checked my tie again. There would be more eyes watching than usual tonight, and

I needed to look like the self-confident prince everyone was expecting. Finding no fault, I left for my father's study.

I nodded at advisors and familiar guards along the way. It was hard to imagine that in less than two weeks, these halls would be flooded with girls. My knock was firm, a request made by Father himself. It seemed there was always a lesson for me to learn.

Knock with authority, Maxon.

Stop pacing all the time, Maxon.

Be faster, smarter, better, Maxon.

"Come in."

I entered the study, and Father briefly moved his eyes from his reflection to acknowledge me. "Ah, there you are. Your mother will be along shortly. Are you ready?"

"Of course," I replied. There was no other acceptable answer.

He reached over and grabbed a small box, placing it in front of me on his desk. "Happy birthday."

I pulled back the silvery paper, revealing a black box. Inside were new cuff links. He was probably too consumed to remember that he'd gotten me cuff links for Christmas. Perhaps that was part of the job. Maybe I'd accidentally get my son the same gift twice when I was king. Of course, to get that far I'd need a wife first.

Wife. I let the word play on my lips without actually saying it aloud. It felt too foreign.

"Thank you, sir. I'll wear them now."

"You'll want to be at your best tonight," he said, tearing

himself away from the mirror. "The Selection will be on everyone's thoughts."

I gave him a tight smile. "Mine included." I debated telling him how anxious I was. He'd been through this, after all. He must have had his own doubts once upon a time.

Evidently, my nerves read on my face.

"Be positive, Maxon. This is meant to be exciting," he urged.

"It is. I'm just a bit shocked at how fast it's all happening." I focused on lacing the metal through the holes on my sleeves.

He laughed. "It seems fast to you, but it's been years in the making on my end."

I narrowed my eyes, looking up from my task. "What do you mean?"

The door opened then, and my mother walked in. In typical fashion, Father lit up for her. "Amberly, you look stunning," he said, going to greet her.

She smiled in that way she always did, as if she couldn't believe anyone would notice her, and embraced my father. "Not too stunning, I hope. I wouldn't want to steal attention." Letting Father go, she came and held me tight. "Happy birthday, son."

"Thanks, Mom."

"Your gift is coming," she whispered, then turned back to Father. "Are we all ready, then?"

"Indeed we are." He held out an arm, she took it, and I walked in their shadows. As always.

★ ★ ★

"About how much longer is it, Your Majesty?" one reporter asked. The light of the video cameras was hot in my face.

"The names are drawn this Friday, and the girls will actually arrive the Friday after that," I answered.

"Are you nervous, sir?" a new voice called.

"About marrying a girl I haven't met yet? All in a day's work." I winked, and the watching crowd chuckled.

"Doesn't it set you on edge at all, Your Majesty?"

I gave up trying to align the question with a face. I just answered in the general direction it came from, hoping to get it right. "On the contrary, I'm very excited." *Sort of.*

"We know you'll make an excellent choice, sir." A camera flash blinded me.

"Hear, hear!" others called.

I shrugged. "I don't know. Any girl who settles for me can't possibly be a sane woman."

They laughed again, and I took that as a good stopping point. "Forgive me, I have family visiting, and I don't wish to be rude."

Turning my back to the reporters and photographers, I took a deep breath. Was the whole evening going to be like this?

I looked around the Great Room—the tables covered in dark blue cloths, the lights burning brightly to show the splendor—and I saw there wasn't much of an escape for me. Dignitaries in one corner, reporters in another—no place I could just be quiet and still. Considering the fact that I was the person being celebrated, one would think that *I* could choose the way in which it happened. It never seemed to work out that way.

No sooner had I escaped the crowd than my father's arm came swooping across my back and gripped my shoulder. The pressure and sudden attention made me tense.

"Smile," he ordered beneath his breath, and I obeyed as he dipped his head in the direction of some of his special guests.

I caught the eye of Daphne, here from France with her father. It was lucky that the timing of the party lined up with our fathers needing to discuss the ongoing trade agreement. As the French king's daughter, our paths had crossed time and time again, and she was perhaps the only person I knew outside of my family with any degree of consistency. It was nice to have one familiar face in the room.

I gave her a nod, and she raised her glass of champagne.

"You can't answer everything so sarcastically. You're the crowned prince. They need you to lead." His hand on my shoulder was tighter than necessary.

"I'm sorry, sir. It's a party, I thought—"

"Well, you thought wrong. By the *Report*, I expect to see you taking this seriously."

He stopped walking and faced me, his eyes gray and steady.

I smiled again, knowing he'd want that for the sake of the crowd. "Of course, sir. A temporary lapse in judgment."

He let his arm drop and pulled his glass of champagne to his lips. "You tend to have a lot of those."

I risked a peek at Daphne and rolled my eyes, at which she

laughed, knowing all too well what I was feeling. Father's gaze followed my eyes across the room.

"Always a pretty one, that girl. Too bad she couldn't be in the lottery."

I shrugged. "She's nice. I never had feelings for her, though."

"Good. That would have been extraordinarily stupid of you."

I dodged the slight. "Besides, I'm looking forward to meeting my true options."

He jumped on the idea, driving me forward once again. "It's about time you made some real choices in your life, Maxon. Some good ones. I'm sure you think my methods are far too harsh, but I need you to see the significance of your position."

I held back a sigh. *I've tried to make choices. You don't really trust me to.*

"Don't worry, Father. I take the task of choosing a wife quite seriously," I answered, hoping my tone gave him some assurance of how much I meant that.

"It's a lot more than finding someone you get along with. For instance, you and Daphne. Very chummy, but she'd be a complete waste." He took another swig, waving at someone behind me.

Again, I controlled my face. Uncomfortable with the direction of the conversation, I put my hands in my pockets and scanned the space. "I should probably make my rounds."

He waved me away, turning his attention back to his

drink, and I left quickly. Try as I might, I wasn't sure what that whole interaction meant. There was no reason for him to be so rude about Daphne when she wasn't even an option.

The Great Room buzzed with excitement. People told me that all of Illéa had been waiting for this moment: the excitement of the new princess, the thrill of me as a soon-to-be king. For the first time, I felt all of that energy and worried it would crush me.

I shook hands and graciously accepted gifts that I didn't need. I quietly asked one of the photographers about his lens, and kissed cheeks of family and friends and my fair share of complete strangers.

Finally I found myself alone for a moment. I surveyed the crowd, sure there was somewhere I ought to be. My eyes found Daphne, and I started walking toward her. I was looking forward to just a few minutes of genuine conversation, but it would have to wait.

"Are you having fun?" Mom asked, stepping into my path.

"Does it look like I am?"

She ran her hands over my already-crisp suit. "Yes."

I smiled. "That's all that really matters."

She tilted her head, a gentle smile on her own face. "Come with me for a second."

I held an arm out for her, which she happily took, and we walked out into the hallway to the sound of cameras clicking.

"Can we do something a bit smaller next year?" I asked.

"Not likely. You'll almost certainly be married by then.

Your wife might want to have a rather elaborate celebration your first year together."

I frowned, something I could get away with in front of her. "Maybe she'll like things quiet, too."

She laughed softly. "Sorry, honey. Any girl who puts her name in for the Selection is looking for a way *out* of quiet."

"Were you?" I wondered aloud. We never talked about her coming here. It was a strange divide between us, but one that I cherished: I was raised in the palace, but she chose to come.

She stopped and faced me, her expression warm. "I was smitten with the face I saw on TV. I daydreamed about your father the same way thousands of girls daydream about you."

I pictured her as a young girl in Honduragua, her hair braided back as she gazed longingly at the television. I could see her sighing every time he had to speak.

"All girls dream of what it would be like to be a princess," she added. "To be swept off their feet and wear a crown . . . it's all I could think about the week before the names were drawn. I didn't realize that it was so much more than that." Her face grew a little sad. "I couldn't guess at the pressure I'd be under or how little privacy I'd have. Still, to be married to your father, to have had you." She swept her hand down my cheek. "This is all those dreams made real."

She held my gaze, smiling, but I could see tears gathering in the corners of her eyes. I had to get her talking again.

"So you have no regrets, then?"

She shook her head. "Not a one. The Selection changed

my life, and I mean that in the best way possible. Which is what I want to talk to you about."

I squinted. "I'm not sure I understand."

She sighed. "I was a Four. I worked in a factory." She held out her hands. "My fingers were dry and cracked, and dirt was caked under my nails. I had no alliances, no status, nothing worthy of making me a princess . . . and yet, here I am."

I stared, still unsure of her point.

"Maxon, this is my gift to you. I promise I will make every effort to see these girls through your eyes. Not the eyes of a queen, or the eyes of your mother, but yours. Even if the girl you choose is of a very low caste, even if others think she has no value, I will always listen to your reasons for wanting her. And I will do my best to support your choice."

After a pause, I understood. "Did Father not have that? Did you not?"

She pulled herself up. "Every girl will come with pros and cons. Some people will choose to focus on the worst in some of your options and the best in others, and it will make no sense to you why they seem so narrow-minded. But I'm here for you, whatever your choice."

"You always have been."

"True," she said, taking my arm. "And I know I'm about to play second fiddle to another woman, as I should. But my love for you will never change, Maxon."

"Nor mine for you." I hoped she could hear the sincerity in my voice. I couldn't imagine a circumstance that would dim my absolute adoration of her.

"I know." With a little nudge, she pushed us back to the party.

As we entered the room to smiles and applause, I considered my mother's words. She was, beyond anyone I knew, incredibly generous. It was a trait I endeavored to adopt myself. So if this was her gift, it must be more necessary than I could understand at the present. My mother never gave a gift thoughtlessly.

CHAPTER 2

PEOPLE LINGERED MUCH LATER THAN I thought was appropriate. That was another sacrifice that came with the privilege, I guessed: no one wanted a palace party to end. Not even when the palace wanted it to.

I'd placed the very drunk dignitary from the German Federation into the care of a guard, thanked all the royal advisors for their gifts, and kissed the hand of nearly every lady who walked through the palace doors. In my eyes, my duty here was done, and I just wanted to spend a few hours in peace. But as I went to escape the lingering partygoers, I was happily stopped by a pair of dark blue eyes.

"You've been avoiding me," Daphne said, her tone playful and the lilt of her accent tickling my ears. There was always something musical about the way she spoke.

"Not at all. It was bit more crowded than I thought it

would be." I looked back at the handful of people still intent on seeing the sun rise through the palace windows.

"Your father, he enjoys making a spectacle."

I laughed. Daphne seemed to understand so many things that I'd never said out loud. Sometimes that made me nervous. Just how much about me could she see without me knowing? "He outdid himself, I think."

She shrugged. "Only until next time."

We stood there in silence, though I sensed she wanted to say more. Biting her lip, she whispered to me. "Could I speak to you in private?"

I nodded, giving her my arm and escorting her to one of the parlors down the hall. She was quiet, saving her words until I shut the doors behind us. Though we often talked in private, the way she was acting made me uneasy.

"You didn't dance with me," she said, sounding hurt.

"I didn't dance at all." Father insisted upon classical musicians this time. While the Fives were very talented, the music they played lent themselves to slower dances. Maybe, if I had wanted to dance, I would have chosen to dance with her. It just felt wrong with everyone asking me questions about my future mystery wife.

She let out a breathy sigh and paced the room. "I'm supposed to go on this date when I get home," she said. "Frederick—that's his name. I've seen him before, of course. He's an excellent rider, and very handsome, too. He's four years older than me, but I think that's one of the reasons Papa likes him."

She looked over her shoulder at me, a little smile on her face.

I gave her a sarcastic grin in return. "And where would we be without our fathers' approval?"

She giggled. "Lost, of course. We'd have no idea how to live."

I laughed back, grateful for someone to joke about it with. It was the only way to deal with it sometimes.

"But yes, Papa approves. Still, I wonder . . ." She dropped her eyes to the floor, suddenly shy.

"You wonder what?"

She stood there a moment, her gaze still focused on the carpet. Finally she focused those deep blue eyes on me. "Do you approve?"

"Of what?"

"Frederick."

I laughed. "I can't really say, can I? I've never met him."

"No," she said, her voice dropping. "Not about the person, but the idea. Do you approve of me dating this man? Possibly marrying him?"

Her face was stone, covering something I didn't understand. I gave a bewildered shrug. "It's not my place to approve. It's hardly even yours," I added, feeling a bit sad for the both of us.

Daphne twisted her hands together, like she was maybe nervous or hurting. What was happening here?

"So it doesn't bother you at all, then? Because if it's not Frederick, it'll be Antoine. And if it's not Antoine, it'll be

Garron. There's a string of men waiting for me, none of them half the friend to me that you are. But, eventually, I'll have to take one as a husband, and you don't care?"

That was gloomy indeed. We scarcely saw each other more than three times in a year. And I might say she was my closest friend, too. How pathetic were we?

I swallowed, searching for the right thing to say. "I'm sure it will all work out."

With no warning whatsoever, tears began streaming down Daphne's face. I looked around the room, trying to find an explanation or solution, feeling more and more uncomfortable every moment.

"Please tell me you're not going to follow through with this, Maxon. You can't," she pleaded.

"What are you talking about?" I asked desperately.

"The Selection! Please, don't marry some stranger. Don't make *me* marry some stranger."

"I have to. That's how it works for princes of Illéa. We marry commoners."

Daphne rushed forward, grabbing my hands. "But I love you. I always have. Please don't marry some other girl without at least asking your father if I could be a choice."

Loved me? Always?

I choked over words, trying to find the right place to start. "Daphne, how . . . I don't know what to say."

"Say you'll ask your father," she pleaded, wiping away her tears hopefully. "Postpone the Selection long enough for us to at least see if it's worth trying. Or let me enter, too. I'll give up my crown."

"Please stop crying," I whispered.

"I can't! Not when I'm about to lose you forever." She buried her head in her hands, sobbing quietly.

I stood there, stone-like, terrified I would make this worse. After a few tense moments, she raised her head. She spoke, staring at nothing.

"You're the only person who really knows me. The only person I feel I truly know myself."

"Knowledge isn't love," I contradicted.

"That's not true, Maxon. We have a history together, and it's about to be broken. All for the sake of tradition." She kept her eyes focused on some invisible space in the center of the room, and I couldn't guess what she was thinking now. Clearly, I was oblivious to her thoughts in general.

Finally Daphne turned her face to me. "Maxon, I beg of you, ask your father. Even if he says no, at least I'll have done everything I could."

Positive that I already knew this to be true, I told her what I must. "You already have, Daphne. This is it." I held out my arms for a moment and let them drop. "This is all it could ever be."

She held my gaze for a long time, knowing as I did that asking my father for such an outrageous request was beyond anything I could truly get away with. I saw her search her mind for an alternative path, but she quickly saw there wasn't one. She was a servant to her crown, I was a servant to mine, and our masters would never cross.

As she nodded, her face crumpled into tears again. She wandered over to a couch and sat down, holding herself. I stayed still, hoping to not cause her any more grief. I longed to make her laugh, but there wasn't anything funny about this. I hadn't known I was capable of breaking a heart.

I certainly didn't like it.

Just then I realized this was about to become common. I would dismiss thirty-four women over the next few months. What if they all reacted this way?

I huffed, exhausted at the thought.

At the sound, she looked up. Slowly, the expression on her face changed.

"Doesn't this hurt you at all?" she demanded. "You're not that good an actor, Maxon."

"Of course it bothers me."

She stood, silently assessing me. "But not for the same reasons it bothers me," she whispered. She walked across the room, her eyes pleading. "Maxon, you love me."

I stayed still.

"Maxon," she said more forcefully, "you love me. You do."

I had to look away, the intensity in her eyes too bright for me. I ran a hand through my hair, trying to put whatever it was I did feel into words.

"I've never seen anyone express their feelings the way you just did. I have no doubt you mean every word, but I can't do that, Daphne."

"That doesn't mean you don't know how to feel it. You

just have no idea how to express it. Your father can be as cold as ice, and your mother hides within herself. You've never seen people love freely, so you don't know how to show it. But you feel it; I know you do. You love me as I love you."

Slowly, I shook my head, fearing another syllable out of my mouth would start everything up again.

"Kiss me," she demanded.

"What?"

"Kiss me. If you can kiss me and still say you don't love me, I'll never mention this again."

I backed away. "No. I'm sorry, I can't."

I didn't want to confess how literal that was. I wasn't sure how many boys Daphne had kissed, but I knew it was more than zero. She'd let the fact she'd been kissed come out a few summers ago when I was in France with her. So there. She had me beat, and there was no way I was going to make an even bigger fool out of myself in this moment.

Her sadness shifted to anger as she backed away from me. She laughed once, no humor in her eyes.

"So this is your answer, then? You're saying no? You're choosing to let me leave?"

I shrugged.

"You're an idiot, Maxon Schreave. Your parents have completely sabotaged you. You could have a thousand girls set before you, and it wouldn't matter. You're too stupid to see love when it stands right in front of you."

She wiped her eyes and straightened her dress. "I hope to God I never see your face again."

The fear in my chest changed, and as she walked away, I grabbed her arm. I didn't want her to be gone forever.

"Daphne, I'm sorry."

"Don't feel sorry for me," she said coldly. "Feel sorry for yourself. You'll find a wife because you have to, but you've already known love and let it go."

She jerked free and left me alone.

Happy birthday to me.

CHAPTER 3

DAPHNE SMELLED LIKE CHERRY BARK and almonds. She'd been wearing the same scent since she turned thirteen. She had it on last night, and I could smell it even as she was wishing she'd never see me again.

She had a scar on her wrist, a scrape she got climbing a tree when she was eleven. It was my fault. She was a bit less ladylike at the time, and I convinced her—well, *challenged* her—to race me to the top of one of the trees on the edge of the garden. I won.

Daphne had a crippling fear of the dark, and since I had fears of my own, I never teased her for it. And she never teased me. Not on anything that really mattered anyway.

She was allergic to shellfish. Her favorite color was yellow. Try as she may, she could not sing to save her life. She could dance, though, so it was probably even more of a disappointment that I didn't ask her to last night.

When I was sixteen she sent me a new camera bag for Christmas. Even though I'd never given any indication that I wanted to get rid of the one I had, it meant so much to me that she was aware of my likes, and I switched it out anyway. I still used it.

I stretched beneath my sheets, turning my head toward where the bag rested. I wondered how much time she'd spent picking out the right one.

Maybe Daphne was right. We had more history than I'd recognized. We'd lived our relationship through scattered visits and sporadic phone calls, so I never would have dreamed it added up to as much as it truly did.

And now she was on a plane back to France, where Frederick was waiting for her.

I climbed out of bed, shrugged off my rumpled shirt and suit pants, and made my way to the shower. As the water washed away the remnants of my birthday, I tried to dismiss my thoughts.

But I couldn't shelve her nagging accusation about the state of my heart. Did I not know love at all? Had I tasted it and cast it off? And if so, how was I supposed to navigate the Selection?

Advisors ran around the palace with stacks of entry forms for the Selection, smiling at me like they knew something I didn't. From time to time, one would pat me on the back or whisper an encouraging remark, as if they sensed that I was suddenly doubting the one thing in my life I'd always counted on, the one thing I hoped for.

"Today's batch is very promising," one would say.

"You're a lucky man," another commented.

But as the entries piled up, all I could think about was Daphne and her cutting words.

I should have been studying the figures of the financial report before me, but instead I studied my father. Had he somehow sabotaged me? Made it so I was missing a fundamental understanding of what it meant to be in a romantic relationship? I'd seen him interact with my mother. There was affection between them, if not passion. Wasn't that enough? Was that what I was meant to be aiming for?

I stared into space, debating. Maybe he thought that if I sought anything more, I'd have a terrible time traversing the Selection. Or perhaps that I'd be disappointed if I didn't find something life-changing. It was probably for the best that I never mentioned I was hoping for just that.

But maybe he had no such designs. People simply are who they are. Father was strict, a sword sharpened under the pressure of running a country that was surviving constant wars and rebel attacks. Mother was a blanket, softened by growing up with nothing, and ever seeking to protect and comfort.

I knew in my core I was more like her than him. Not something I minded, but Father did.

So maybe making me slow about expressing myself was intentional, part of the process intended to harden me.

You're too stupid to see love when it stands right in front of you.

"Snap out of it, Maxon." I whipped my head toward my father's voice.

"Sir?"

His face was tired. "How many times do I have to tell you? The Selection is about making a solid, rational choice, not another opportunity for you to daydream."

An advisor walked into the room, handing a letter to Father as I straightened the stack of papers, tapping them against the desk. "Yes, sir."

He read the paper, and I looked at him one last time.

Maybe.

No.

At the end of the day, no. He wanted to make me a man, not a machine.

With a grunt, he crumpled the paper and threw it in the trash. "Damn rebels."

I spent the better part of the next morning working in my room, away from prying eyes. I felt much more productive when I was alone, and if I wasn't productive, at least I wasn't being chastised. I guessed that wouldn't last all day, based on the invitation I received.

"You called for me?" I asked, stepping into my father's private office.

"There you are," Father said, his eyes wide. He rubbed his hands together. "Tomorrow's the day."

I drew in a breath. "Yes. Do we need to go over the format for the *Report*?"

"No, no." He put a hand on my back to move me forward, and I straightened instantly, following his lead. "It'll be simple enough. Introduction, a little chat with Gavril, and then we'll broadcast the names and faces of the girls."

I nodded. "Sounds . . . easy."

When we reached the edge of his desk, he placed his hand on a thick stack of folders. "These are them."

I looked down. Stared. Swallowed.

"Now, about twenty-five or so have rather obvious qualities that would be perfect for a new princess. Excellent families, ties to other countries that might be very valuable. Some of them are just extraordinarily beautiful." Uncharacteristically, he playfully elbowed my rib, and I stepped to the side. None of this was a game. "Sadly, not all of the provinces offered up anyone worth note. So, to make it all appear a bit more random, we used those areas to add in a bit more diversity. You'll see we got a few Fives in the mix. Nothing below that, though. We have to have *some* standards."

I played his words in my head again. All this time, I thought it would be fate or destiny . . . but it was just him.

He ran his thumb down the stack, and the edges of the papers smacked together.

"Do you want a peek?" he asked.

I looked at the pile again. Names, photos, and lists of accomplishments. All the essential details were there. Still, I knew for a fact the form didn't ask anything about what made them laugh or urge them to spill their darkest secret. Here sat a compilation of attributes, not people. And based on those statistics, they were my only choices.

"You chose them?" I pulled my eyes from the papers and looked to him.

"Yes."

"*All* of them?"

"Essentially," he said with a smile. "Like I said, there are a few there for the sake of the show, but I think you've got a very promising lot. Far better than mine."

"Did your father choose for you?"

"Some. But it was different then. Why do you ask?"

I thought back. "This is what you meant, wasn't it? When you said it was years of work on your end?"

"Well, we had to make sure certain girls would be of age, and in some provinces we had several options. But, trust me, you're going to love them."

"Am I?"

Love them? As if he cared. As if this wasn't just another way to push the crown, the palace, and himself ahead.

Suddenly, his offhand comment about Daphne being a waste made sense. He didn't care if I was close to her because she was charming or good company; he cared that she was *France*. Not even a person to him. And since he basically had what he needed from France, she was useless in his eyes. Had she proven valuable, I had no doubt that he would have been willing to throw a beloved tradition out this window.

He sighed. "Don't mope. I thought you'd be excited. Don't you even want to look?"

I straightened my suit coat. "As you've said, this is nothing to daydream over. I'll see them when everyone else does. If you'll excuse me, I need to finish reading the amendment you drafted."

I walked away without waiting for approval, but I felt certain my answer would be a sufficient enough excuse to let me leave.

Maybe it wasn't exactly sabotage, but it certainly felt like a trap. To find one girl I liked out of dozens he handpicked? How was that supposed to happen?

I told myself to calm down. He picked Mom, after all, and she was a wonderful, beautiful, intelligent person. But that happened without this level of interference, it seemed. And things were different now, or so he claimed.

Between Daphne's words, Father's interloping, and my own growing fears, I was dreading the Selection like never before.

CHAPTER 4

WITH JUST FIVE MINUTES TO go before my entire future unfolded in front of me, I found myself prepared to vomit at a moment's notice.

A very kind makeup woman was dabbing sweat off my brow.

"Are you all right, sir?" she asked, moving the cloth.

"I was just lamenting that with all the lipstick you have over there, not a one appears to be my shade." Mom said that sometimes: *not my shade*. Not really sure what it meant.

She giggled, as did Mom and her makeup woman.

"I think I'm good," I told the girl, looking in the mirrors set up in the back of the studio. "Thank you."

"Me, too," Mom said, and the two young women walked away.

I toyed with a container, trying not to think about the passing seconds.

"Maxon, sweetie, are you really okay?" Mom asked, looking not at me but at my reflection. I looked back at hers.

"It's just . . . it's . . ."

"I know. It's nerve-racking for everyone involved, but at the end of the day, it's just hearing the names of a few girls. That's all."

I inhaled slowly and nodded. That was one way to look at it. Names. That was all that was happening. Just a list of names and nothing more.

I drew in another breath.

It was a good thing I hadn't eaten much today.

I turned and walked to my seat on the set, where Father was already waiting.

He shook his head. "Get it together. You look like hell."

"How did you do this?" I begged.

"I faced it with confidence because I was the prince. As will you. Need I remind you that you're the prize?" His face looked tired again, like I ought to have already grasped this. "They're competing for you, not the other way around. Your life isn't changing at all, except you'll have to deal with a couple of overly excited females for a few weeks."

"What if I don't like any of them?"

"Then pick the one you hate the least. Preferably one that's useful. Don't worry on that count, though; I'll help."

If he intended that to be a calming thought, he failed.

"Ten seconds," someone called, and my mother came to her seat, giving me a comforting wink.

"Remember to smile," Father prompted, and turned to face the cameras confidently.

Suddenly the anthem was playing and people were speaking. I realized I ought to be paying attention, but all of my focus was driven toward keeping a calm and happy expression on my face.

I didn't register much until I heard Gavril's familiar voice.

"Good evening, Your Majesty," he said, and I swallowed in fear before realizing he was addressing my father.

"Gavril, always good to see you."

"Looking forward to the announcement?"

"Ah, yes. I was in the room yesterday as a few were drawn; all very lovely girls." He was so smooth, so natural.

"So you know who they are already?" Gavril asked excitedly.

"Just a few, just a few." A complete fabrication, pulled off with incredible ease.

"Did he happen to share any of this information with you, sir?" Now Gavril was talking to me, the glint from his lapel pin sparkling in the bright lights as he moved.

Father turned to me, his eyes reminding me to smile. I did so and answered.

"Not at all. I'll see them when everyone else does." Ugh, I should have said *the ladies*, not *them*. They were guests, not pets. I discreetly wiped the sweat from my palms on my pants.

"Your Majesty," Gavril said, moving to my mother. "Any advice for the Selected?"

I watched her. How long did it take for her to become so poised, so flawless? Or was she always that way? A bashful tilt of her head and even Gavril melted.

"Enjoy your last night as an average girl. Tomorrow, no matter what, your life will be different forever." *Yes, ladies, yours and mine both.* "And it's old advice, but it's good: be yourself."

"Wise words, my queen, wise words." He turned with a wide sweep of his arm to the cameras. "And with that, let us reveal the thirty-five young ladies chosen for the Selection. Ladies and gentlemen, please join me in congratulating the following Daughters of Illéa."

I watched the monitors as the national emblem popped up, leaving a small box in the corner showing my face. What? They were going to watch me the whole time?

Mom put her hand on mine, just out of the sight of the camera. I breathed in. Then out. Then in again.

Just a bunch of names. Not a big deal. Not like they were announcing one, and she was it.

"Miss Elayna Stoles of Hansport, Three," Gavril read off a card. I worked hard to smile a little brighter. "Miss Tuesday Keeper of Waverly, Four," he continued.

Still looking excited, I bent toward Father. "I feel sick," I whispered.

"Just breathe," he answered back through his teeth. "You should have looked yesterday; I knew it."

"Miss Fiona Castley of Paloma, Three."

I looked over to Mom. She smiled. "Very pretty."

"Miss America Singer of Carolina, Five."

I heard the word *Five* and realized that must have been one of Father's throwaway picks. I didn't even catch the picture, as my new plan was to stare just above the monitors and smile.

"Miss Mia Blue of Ottaro, Three."

It was too much to absorb. I'd learn their names and faces later, when the nation wasn't watching.

"Miss Celeste Newsome of Clermont, Two." I raised my eyebrows, not that I even saw her face. If she was a Two, she must be an important one, so I'd better look impressed.

"Clarissa Kelley of Belcourt, Two."

As the list rolled on, I smiled to the point that my cheeks ached. All I could think of was how much this meant to me—how a huge part of my life was falling into place right now—and I couldn't even rejoice in it. If I'd picked the names myself out of a bowl in a private room, saw their faces on my own, before anyone else, how that would have changed everything in this moment.

These girls were mine, the only thing in the world that might ever truly feel that way.

And then they weren't.

"And there you have it!" Gavril announced. "Those are our beautiful Selection candidates. Over the next week they will be prepared for their trip to the palace, and we will eagerly await their arrival. Tune in next Friday for a special edition of the *Report* devoted exclusively to getting to know these spectacular women. Prince Maxon," he said, turning my way, "I congratulate you, sir. Such a stunning group of young women."

"I'm quite speechless," I replied, not lying in the slightest.

"Don't worry, sir, I'm sure the girls will do most of the talking once they arrive next Friday. And to you"—he spoke to the camera—"don't forget to stay tuned for all the latest Selection updates right here on the Public Access Channel. Good night, Illéa!"

The anthem played, the lights went down, and I finally let my posture relax.

Father stood and gave me a firm and startling pat on the back. "Well done. That was a vast deal better than I thought you'd fare."

"I have no clue what just happened."

He laughed along with a handful of advisors who were lingering on set. "I told you, son, you're the prize. There's no need to be stressed. Don't you agree, Amberly?"

"I assure you, Maxon, the ladies have much more to worry about than you do," she confirmed, rubbing my arm.

"Exactly," Father said. "Now, I'm starving. Let's enjoy our last few peaceful meals together."

I stood, walking slowly, and Mom kept my pace.

"That was a blur," I whispered.

"We'll get the photos and applications to you so you can study them at your leisure. It's just like getting to know anyone. Treat it like spending time with any of your other friends."

"I don't have very many friends, Mom."

She gave me a knowing smile. "Yes, it's confining in here," she agreed. "Well, think about Daphne."

"What about her?" I asked, a bit on edge.

Mom didn't notice. "She's a girl, and you two have always been friendly. Pretend it's just like that."

I faced forward. Without realizing it, she soothed a huge fear in my heart while stoking another.

Since our fight, whenever I thought about Daphne, it wasn't about how she might be getting along with Frederick right now, or how much I missed her company. All I thought about were her accusations.

If I was in love with her, certainly it would be all of her attributes that filled my head. Or tonight, as the Selected girls were listed, I would have wished her name were in there somewhere.

Maybe Daphne was right, and I didn't know how to properly show love. But even if that were the case, I knew with a growing certainty that I didn't love her.

A corner of my soul rejoiced in knowing that I wasn't missing out on something. I could enter the Selection with no restraints on my affection. But in another space, I mourned. At least if I had misunderstood my emotions, I could boast at the fact that once upon a time, I'd been in love, that I knew what it felt like. But I still had no clue. I supposed it was always meant to be that way.

CHAPTER 5

IN THE END, I DIDN'T look at the applications. I had a lot of reasons to not bother, but ultimately, I convinced myself it was best if it was a clean slate for all of us once we were introduced. Besides, if Father had pored over all the candidates in detail, maybe I didn't want to.

I held a comfortable distance between the Selection and myself . . . until the event crossed my threshold.

Friday morning, I was walking along the third floor, and I heard the musical laugh of two girls on the open stairwell of the second floor. A perky voice gushed, "Can you believe we're here?" and they burst into giggles again.

I cursed aloud and ran into the closest room, because it had been stressed to me over and over again that I was to meet the girls all at once on Saturday. No one told me why it was so important, but I believed it had something to do with their makeovers. If a Five stepped into the palace without any sort of help, well, I couldn't say she'd have much of a chance. Maybe it was to make everything fair. I discreetly left the room I'd ducked into and went back to my own, trying to forget the incident altogether.

But then a second time as I was walking to drop something off in Father's office, I heard the floating voice of a girl I did not know, and it sent a jolt of anxiety through my entire being. I went back to my room and cleaned all of my camera lenses meticulously and reorganized all my equipment. I busied myself until nightfall, when I knew the girls would be in their rooms, and I could walk.

It was one of those traits that tended to get on Father's nerves. He said it made him nervous that I moved around so much. What could I say? I thought better on my feet.

The palace was quiet. If I didn't know better, I wouldn't have guessed that we had so much company. Maybe things wouldn't be so different if I didn't focus on the change.

As I made my way to the end of the hall, I was faced with all the *what if*s that were plaguing me. What if none of the girls was someone I could love? What if none of them loved me? What if my soul mate was bypassed because someone more valuable was chosen from her province?

I sat down at the top of the stairs and put my head in my hands. How was I supposed to do this? How was I meant to find someone who I loved, who loved me, who my parents approved of, and the people adored? Not to mention someone who was smart, attractive, and accomplished, someone I could present to all the presidents and ambassadors who came our way.

I told myself to pull it together, to think about the positive *what ifs*. What if I had a spectacular time getting to know these ladies? What if they were all charming and funny and beautiful? What if the very girl I cared for the most would appease my father beyond any expectations either of us had? What if my perfect match was lying in her bed right now, hoping the best for me?

Maybe . . . maybe this could be everything I'd dreamed it would be, back before it became all too real. This was my chance to find a partner. For so long, Daphne was the only person I could confide in; no one else quite understood our lives. But now, I could welcome someone else into my world, and it would be better than anything I'd ever had before because . . . because she would be mine.

And I would be hers. We would be there for each other. She would be what my mother was to my father: a source of comfort, the calm that grounded him. And I could be her guide, her protector.

I stood and moved downstairs, feeling confident. I just had to hold on to this feeling. I told myself that this was what the Selection would really be for me. It was hope.

By the time I hit the first floor, I was actually smiling. I wasn't relaxed, exactly, but I was determined.

" . . . outside," someone gasped, the fragile voice echoing down the hallway. What was happening?

"Miss, you need to get back to your room now." I squinted

down the hall and saw in a patch of moonlight that a guard was blocking a girl—a girl!—from the doorway. It was dark, so I couldn't make out much of her face, but she had brilliant red hair, like honey and roses and the sun all together.

"Please." She was looking more and more distressed as she stood there shaking. I walked closer, trying to decide what to do.

The guard said something I couldn't make out. I kept walking, trying to make sense of the scene.

"I . . . I can't breathe," she said, falling into the guard's arms as he dropped his staff to catch her. He seemed kind of irritated about it.

"Let her go!" I ordered, finally getting to them. Rules be damned, I couldn't let this girl be hurt.

"She collapsed, Your Majesty," the guard explained. "She wanted to go outside."

I knew the guards were just trying to keep us all safe, but what could I do? "Open the doors," I commanded.

"But . . . Your Majesty . . ."

I fixed him with a serious gaze. "Open the doors and let her go. Now!"

"Right away, Your Highness."

The guard by the door went to work opening the lock, and I watched the girl sway slightly in the other's arms as she tried to stand. The moment the double doors opened, a rush of warm, sweet Angeles wind enveloped us. As soon as she felt it on her bare arms, she was moving.

I went to the door and watched as she staggered through

the garden, her bare feet making dull sounds on the smoothed gravel. I'd never seen a girl in a nightgown before, and while this particular young lady wasn't exactly graceful at the moment, it was still strangely inviting.

I realized the guards were watching her, too, and that bothered me.

"As you were," I said in a low voice. They cleared their throats and turned back to face the hallway. "Stay here unless I call for you," I instructed, and walked into the garden.

I had a hard time seeing her, but I could hear her. She was breathing heavily, and sounded almost like she was weeping. I hoped that wasn't the case. Finally I saw her collapse in the grass with her arms and head resting on a stone bench.

She didn't seem to notice that I'd approached, so I stood there a moment, waiting for her to look up. After a while I was starting to feel a little awkward. I figured she'd at least want to thank me, so I spoke.

"Are you all right, my dear?"

"I am *not* your dear," she said angrily as she whipped her head to look at me. She was still hidden by shadows, but her hair flashed in the sliver of moonlight that made its way through the clouds.

Still, face lit or hidden, I got the full intention of her words. Where was the gratitude? "What have I done to offend you? Did I not just give you the very thing you asked for?"

She didn't answer me, but turned away, back to her crying. Why did women have such a high inclination to tears? I didn't want to be rude, but I had to ask.

"Excuse me, dear, are you going to keep crying?"

"Don't call me that! I am no more dear to you than the thirty-four other strangers you have here in your cage."

I smiled to myself. One of my many worries was that these girls would be in a constant state of presenting the best sides of themselves, trying to impress me. I kept dreading that I'd spend weeks getting to know someone, think she was the one, and then after the wedding, some new person would come to the surface who I couldn't stand.

And here was one who didn't care who I was. She was scolding me!

I circled her as I thought about what she said. I wondered if my habit of walking would bother her. If it did, would she say so?

"That is an unfair statement. You are all dear to me," I said. Yes, I'd been avoiding anything having to do with the Selection, but that didn't mean the girls weren't precious in my eyes. "It is simply a matter of discovering who shall be the dearest."

"Did you really just use the word *shall*?" she asked incredulously.

"I'm afraid I did," I answered with a chuckle. "Forgive me, it's a product of my education." She muttered something unintelligible. "I'm sorry?"

"It's ridiculous!" she yelled. My, she had a temper. Father must not know much about this one. Certainly, no girl with this disposition would have made it into the pool if he had. It was lucky for her that I was the one who came upon her in her distress, and not him. She would have been sent home about five minutes ago.

"What is?" I inquired, though I was sure she was referencing this very moment. I'd never experienced anything quite like this.

"This contest! The whole thing! Haven't you ever loved anyone at all? Is this really how you want to pick a wife? Are you really so shallow?"

That stung. Shallow? I went to sit on the bench, so it would be easier to talk. I wanted this girl, whoever she was, to understand where I was coming from, what things looked like from my end. I tried not to get distracted by the curve of her waist and hip and leg, even the look of her bare foot.

"I can see how I would seem that way, how this whole thing could seem like it's nothing more than cheap entertainment," I said, nodding. "But in my world, I am very guarded. I don't meet very many women. The ones I do are daughters of diplomats, and we usually have very little to discuss. And that's when we manage to speak the same language."

I smiled, thinking of the awkward moments when I had to sit through long dinners in silence next to young women who I was meant to entertain, and failing dismally because the translators were busy talking politics. I looked to the girl, expecting her to laugh along with me for my trouble. When her tight lips refused to smile, I cleared my throat and moved on.

"Circumstances being what they are," I said, fidgeting

with my hands, "I haven't had the opportunity to fall in love." She seemed to forget I wasn't really allowed to until now. Then I was curious. Hoping I wasn't alone, I voiced my most intimate question. "Have you?"

"Yes," she said. She sounded both proud and sad in a single word.

"Then you have been quite lucky."

I looked at the grass for a moment. I continued on, not wanting to linger on my rather embarrassing lack of experience.

"My mother and father were married this way and are quite happy. I hope to find happiness, too. To find a woman who all of Illéa can love, someone to be my companion and to help entertain the leaders of other nations. Someone who will befriend my friends and be my confidante. I'm ready to find my wife."

Even I could hear the desperation, the hope, the longing. The doubt crept back in. What if no one here could love me?

No, I told myself, *this will be a good thing.*

I looked down at this girl, who seemed desperate in her own way. "Do you really·feel like this is a cage?"

"Yes, I do," she breathed. Then, a second later, "Your Majesty."

I laughed. "I've felt that way more than once myself. But, you must admit, it is a very beautiful cage."

"For you," she shot back skeptically. "Fill your beautiful cage with thirty-four other men all fighting over the same thing. See how nice it is then."

"Have there really been arguments over me? Don't you all realize I'm the one doing the choosing?" I didn't know whether to feel excited or worried, but it was interesting to think about. Maybe if someone really wanted me that much, I'd want them, too.

"Actually, that was unfair," she added. "They're fighting over two things. Some fight for you; others fight for the crown. And they all think they've already figured out what to say and do so your choice will be obvious."

"Ah, yes. The man or the crown. I'm afraid some cannot tell the difference." I shook my head and stared into the grass.

"Good luck there," she said comically.

But there was nothing comical about it. Here was another one of my biggest fears being confirmed. Again my curiosity overwhelmed me, though I was sure she would lie.

"Which do you fight for?"

"Actually, I'm here by mistake."

"Mistake?" How was that possible? If she put her name in, and it was drawn, and she willingly came here . . .

"Yes. I sort of—well, it's a long story," she said. I would have to learn what that was all about eventually. "And now . . . I'm here. And I'm not fighting. My plan is to enjoy the food until you kick me out."

I couldn't help myself. I burst out laughing. This girl was the antithesis of everything I'd been expecting. Waiting to be kicked out? Here for the food? I was, surprisingly, enjoying this. Maybe it would all be as simple as Mom said it would be, and I could get to know the candidates over time, like I did with Daphne.

"What are you?" I asked. She couldn't be more than a Four if she was so excited about the food.

"I'm sorry?" she asked, not catching my meaning.

I didn't want to be insulting, so I started high. "A Two? Three?"

"Five."

So this was one of the Fives. I knew Father wouldn't be thrilled about me being friendly with her, but after all, he was the one who let her in. "Ah, yes, then food would probably be good motivation to stay." I chuckled again, and tried to find out the name of this entertaining young woman. "I'm sorry, I can't read your pin in the dark."

She gave a slight shake of her head. If she asked why I didn't know her name yet I wondered which would sound better: a lie—that I had far too much work to do to put them to memory at the moment—or the truth—that I was so nervous about all this, I'd been putting it off until the last second.

Which I suddenly realized I'd just passed.

"I'm America."

"Well, that's perfect," I said with a laugh. Based on her name alone, I couldn't believe she'd made the cut. That was the name of the old country, a stubborn and flawed land we rebuilt into something strong. Then again, maybe that was why Father let her in: to show he had no fear or worries about our past, even if the rebels clung to it foolishly.

For me, there was something musical about the word. "America, my dear, I do hope you find something in this cage worth fighting for. After all this, I can only imagine what it would be like to see you actually try."

I left the bench and knelt beside her, taking her hand. She was looking at our fingers and not into my eyes, and thank goodness for that. If she were, she'd have seen how absolutely floored I was the first time I finally, truly saw her. The clouds moved at just the right moment, fully lighting her face by the moon. As if it weren't enough that she was willing to stand up to me and clearly unafraid to be herself, she was dazzlingly beautiful.

Underneath thick lashes were eyes blue as ice, something cool to balance out the flames in her hair. Her cheeks were smooth and slightly blushed from crying. And her lips, soft and pink, slightly parted as she studied our hands.

I felt a strange flutter in my chest, like the glow of a fireplace or the warmth of the afternoon. It stayed there for a moment, playing with my pulse.

I mentally chastised myself. How typical to become so infatuated with the first girl I was ever allowed to actually have any sort of feelings for. It was foolish, too quick to be real, and I pushed the warmth away. All the same, I didn't want to dismiss her. Time might prove that she was someone worth having in the running. America was clearly someone I'd need to win over, and that might take time. But I would start right now.

"If it would make you happy, I could let the staff know

you prefer the garden. Then you can come out here at night without being manhandled by the guard. I would prefer if you had one nearby, though." No need to worry her with just how often we were attacked. So long as a guard was close, she should be fine.

"I don't . . . I don't think I want anything from you." She gently pulled her hand away and looked at the grass.

"As you wish." I was a little disappointed. What horrible thing had I done to make her push me away? Maybe this girl was unwinnable. "Will you be heading inside soon?"

"Yes," she whispered.

"Then I'll leave you with your thoughts. There will be a guard near the door waiting for you." I wanted her to take her time, but I dreaded some unexpected assault hurting any of the girls, even this girl who seemed to have developed a serious distaste for me.

"Thank you, um, Your Majesty." I heard a sort of vulnerability in her voice, and realized that maybe it wasn't me. Maybe she was just overwhelmed by everything that was happening to her. How could I blame her for that? I decided to risk rejection again.

"Dear America, will you do me a favor?" I took her hand once more, and she looked up to me with a skeptical face. There was something about those eyes on me, like she was searching for truth in mine and would have it at all costs.

"Maybe."

Her tone gave me hope, and I grinned. "Don't mention this to the others. Technically, I'm not supposed to meet you until tomorrow, and I don't want anyone getting upset." I gave a light snort, and I immediately wished I could take it back. Sometimes I had the *worst* laugh. "Though I wouldn't call you yelling at me anything close to a romantic tryst, would you?"

Finally America gave me a playful smirk. "Not at all!" She paused and let out a breath. "I won't tell."

"Thank you." I should have been happy enough with her smile, should have walked away at that. But something in me—perhaps being raised to always push forward, to succeed—urged me to take one step more. I pulled her hand to my lips and kissed it. "Good night." I left before she had a chance to chastise me or I had an opportunity to do anything else stupid.

I wanted to look back and see her expression, but if it was something in the area of disgust, I didn't think I could bear it. If Father could read my thoughts right now, he'd be less than pleased. By now, after everything, I ought to be tougher than this.

When I got to the doors, I turned to the guards. "She needs a moment. If she's not in within half an hour, *kindly* urge her to come inside." I met both of their eyes, making sure they grasped the concept. "It would also behoove you to refrain from mentioning this to anyone. Understood?"

They nodded, and I made my way to the main stairwell. As I walked I heard one guard whisper, "What's *behoove*?"

I rolled my eyes and continued up the stairs. Once I made it to the third floor, I practically ran to my room. I had a huge balcony that overlooked the gardens. I wasn't going to step outside and let her know I was watching, but I did go to the window and pull back the curtain.

She stayed maybe ten minutes or so, seeming calmer by the minute. I watched as she wiped her face, brushed off her nightgown, and headed inside. I debated hopping into the hallway on the second floor so we could accidentally-on-purpose meet again. But I thought better of it. She was upset tonight, probably not herself. If I was going to have a chance at all, I'd have to wait until tomorrow.

Tomorrow . . . when thirty-four other girls would be placed before me. Oh, I was an idiot to wait so long. I went to my desk and dug out the stack of files about the girls, studying their pictures. I didn't know whose idea it was to put the names on the back, but that was far less than helpful. I grabbed a pen and transcribed the names to the front. Hannah, Anna . . . how was I supposed to keep that straight? Jenna, Janelle, and Camille . . . seriously? That was going to be a disaster. I had to learn at least a few. Then I'd just rely on the pins until I got the names straight.

Because I could do this. I could do it well. I had to. I had to prove, finally, that I could lead, make decisions. How else would anyone trust me as their king? How would the king himself trust me at all?

I focused on standouts. Celeste . . . I remembered the name. One of my advisors had mentioned she was a model and showed me a picture of her in a bathing suit on the glossy pages of a magazine. She was probably the sexiest candidate, and I certainly wouldn't hold that against her. Lyssa jumped out at me, but not in a good way. Unless she had a winning personality, she wasn't even in the running. Maybe that was a bit shallow, but was it so bad that I wanted someone attractive? Ah, Elise. Based on the exotic slant of her eyes, she was the girl Father had mentioned who had family in New Asia. She'd be in the running on that alone.

America.

I studied her picture. Her smile was absolutely radiant.

What made her smile so brightly, then? Was it me? Had whatever she felt for me that day passed? She didn't seem very happy to meet me. But . . . she did smile in the end.

Tomorrow I would have to start fresh with her. I wasn't sure of what I was looking for, but so much of what seemed *right* was staring back at me in that photograph. Maybe it was her will or her honesty, maybe it was the soft skin on the back of her hand or her perfume . . . but I knew, with a singular clarity, that I wanted her to like me.

How exactly was I supposed to do that?

CHAPTER 6

I HELD THE BLUE TIE up. No. The tan? No. Was I going to have this much trouble getting dressed every day?

I wanted to make a good first impression with these girls—and a good second impression with one—and apparently I was convinced this all hung on picking out the right tie. I sighed. These girls were already turning me into a puddle of stupid.

I tried to follow my mother's advice and be myself, flaws and all. Going with the first tie I'd picked up, I finished getting dressed and smoothed my hair back.

I walked out the door and found my parents by the stairwell having a hushed conversation. I debated taking a back route, not wanting to interrupt them, but my mother waved me over.

Once I reached them, she started tugging on my sleeves,

then moved to my back to smooth my coat. "Remember," she said, "they're swarming with nerves, and the thing to do right now is make them feel at home."

"Act like a prince," Father urged. "Remember who you are."

"There's no rush to make a decision." Mom touched my tie. "That's a nice one."

"But don't keep anyone around if you know you don't want them. The sooner we get to the true candidates, the better."

"Be polite."

"Be confident."

"Just talk."

Father sighed. "This isn't a joke. Remember that."

Mom held me at arm's length. "You're going to be fantastic." She pulled me in for a big hug, and backed away to restraighten everything.

"All right, son. Go on," Father said, gesturing to the stairs.

"We'll be waiting in the dining hall."

I felt dizzy. "Um, yes. Thank you."

I paused for a minute to catch my breath. I knew they were trying to help, but they'd managed to throw off any sense of calm I'd built. I reminded myself that this was just me saying hello, that the girls were hoping this would work out as much as I was.

And then I remembered that I was going to get to speak to America again. At the very least, that should be entertaining. With that in mind I breezed down the stairs to the first floor and made my way to the Great Room. I took one deep breath and gave a knock on the door before pulling it open.

There, past the guards, waited the collection of girls. Cameras flashed, capturing both their reactions and mine. I smiled at their hopeful faces, feeling calmer just because they all looked so pleased to be here.

"Your Majesty." I turned and caught Silvia coming up from her curtsy. I nearly forgot that she would be there, instructing them in protocol the way she instructed me when I was younger.

"Hello, Silvia. If you don't mind, I would like to introduce myself to these young women."

"Of course," she said breathlessly, bending again. She could be so dramatic sometimes.

I surveyed the faces, looking for the flame of her hair. It took a moment, as I was a bit distracted by the light glinting off nearly every wrist, ear, and neck in the room. I finally found her, a few rows in on the end, looking at me with a different expression than the others. I smiled, but instead of smiling back, she looked confused.

"Ladies, if you don't mind," I started, "one at a time, I'll be calling you over to meet with me. I'm sure you're all eager to eat, as am I. So I won't take up too much of your time. Do forgive me if I'm slow with names; there are quite a few of you."

Some of the girls giggled, and I was happy to realize I could identify more of them than I thought I would. I went to the young lady in the front corner, and extended my hand. She took it enthusiastically, and we walked over to the couches that I knew would be set up specifically for this purpose.

Sadly, Lyssa was no more attractive in person than she was in her picture. Still, she deserved the benefit of the doubt, so we spoke all the same.

"Good morning, Lyssa."

"Good morning, Your Majesty." She smiled so widely, it looked like it must hurt her to do so.

"How are you finding the palace?"

"It's beautiful. I've never seen anything so beautiful. It's really beautiful here. Gosh, I already said that, didn't I?"

I answered with a smile. "It's quite all right. I'm glad you're so pleased. What do you do at home?"

"I'm a Five. My whole family works exclusively in sculpting. You have some incredible pieces here. Really beautiful."

I tried to seem interested, but she didn't engage me at all. Still, what if I passed on someone for no good reason?

"Thank you. Um, how many siblings do you have?"

After a few minutes of conversation in which she used the word *beautiful* no less than twelve times, I knew that there was nothing else I wanted to know about this girl.

It was time for me to move on, but it seemed so cruel to keep her here knowing there was no chance for us. I decided that I was going to start making cuts here and now. It would be kinder to the girls, and maybe also impress Father. After all, he did say he wanted me to make some real choices in my life.

"Lyssa, thank you so much for your time. Once I'm done with everyone, would you mind staying a little longer so I could speak with you?"

She blushed. "Absolutely."

We rose, and I felt awful knowing that she assumed that request meant something it didn't. "Would you please send the next young lady over?"

She nodded and curtsied before she went to get the girl beside her, who I recognized immediately as Celeste Newsome. It would take a dim man indeed to forget that face.

"Good morning, Lady Celeste."

"Good morning, Your Majesty," she said as she curtsied. Her voice was sugary, and I realized right away that many of these girls might have a hold on me. Maybe all this worry about not being able to love any of them wasn't the true problem. Maybe I'd fall for all of them and never be able to choose.

I motioned for her to sit across from me. "I understand you model."

"I do," she answered brightly, thrilled to see I already knew this about her. "Primarily clothing. I've been told I have a good shape for it."

Of course, at those words, I was forced to look at said shape, and there was no denying just how striking she was.

"Do you enjoy your work?"

"Oh, yes. It's amazing how photography can capture just a split second of something exquisite."

I lit up. "Absolutely. I don't know if you're aware, but I'm very into photography myself."

"Really? We should do a shoot sometime."

"That would be wonderful." Ah! This was going better than I thought. Within ten minutes I'd already weeded out a definite no and found someone with a common interest.

I could have probably gone on for another hour with Celeste, but if we were ever going to eat, I really needed to hurry.

"My dear, I'm so sorry to cut this short, but I have to meet everyone this morning," I apologized.

"Of course." She stood. "I'm looking forward to finishing our conversation. Hopefully soon."

The way she looked at me . . . I didn't know the proper words for it. It sent a blush to my face, and I nodded my head in a tiny bow to cover it. I took some deep breaths, focusing myself on the next girl.

Bariel, Emmica, Tiny, and several others passed through. So far, most of them were pleasant and composed. But I was hoping for so much more than that.

It took five more girls until anything really interesting happened. As I stepped forward to greet the slim brunette coming my way, she extended her hand. "Hi, I'm Kriss."

I stared at her open palm and was prepared to shake it before she pulled it back.

"Oh, darn! I meant to curtsy!" She did, shaking her head as she rose.

I laughed.

"I feel so silly. The very first thing, and I got it wrong." But she smiled it off, and it was actually kind of charming.

"Don't worry, my dear," I said, gesturing for her to sit. "There's been much worse."

"Really?" she whispered, excited by the news.

"I won't go into details, but yes. At least you were attempting to be polite."

Her eyes widened, and she looked over at the girls, wondering who might have been rude to me. I was glad I'd chosen to be discreet, seeing as it was *last night* someone called me shallow, and that was a secret.

"So, Kriss, tell me about your family," I began.

She shrugged. "Typical, I guess. I live with my mom and dad, and they're both professors. I think I'd like to teach as well, though I dabble in writing. I'm an only child, and I'm finally coming to terms with it. I begged my parents for a sibling for years. They never caved."

I smiled. It was tough being alone.

"I'm sure it was because they wanted to focus all their love on you."

She giggled. "Is that what your parents told you?"

I froze. No one had asked a question about *me* yet.

"Well, not exactly. But I understand how you feel," I hedged. I was about to go into the rest of my rehearsed questions, but she beat me to it.

"How are you feeling today?"

"All right. It's a bit overwhelming," I blurted, being a bit too honest.

"At least you don't have to wear the dresses," she commented.

"But think of how fun it would have been if I had."

A laugh tumbled out of her mouth, and I echoed it. I imagined Kriss next to Celeste, and thought of them as opposites. There was something entirely wholesome about her. I left our time together without a complete impression of her, since she kept pointing the conversation back to me, but I recognized that she was good, in the best sense of the word.

It was nearly an hour before I got to America. In the time between the first girls and her, I'd already met three solid standouts, including Celeste and Kriss, who I knew would be favorites with the public. However, the girl just before her, Ashley, was so dismally wrong for me she washed all of those thoughts out of my head. When America stood up and moved toward me, she was the only person on my mind.

Something about her eyes was mischievous, whether she meant it or not. I thought of how she acted last night, and I realized she was a walking rebellion.

"America, is it?" I joked as she approached.

"Yes, it is. And I know I've heard your name before, but could you remind me?"

I laughed and invited her to sit. Leaning in, I whispered, "Did you sleep well, my dear?"

Her eyes said I was playing with fire, but her lips carried a smile. "I am still not your dear. But yes. Once I calmed down, I slept very well. My maids had to pull me out of bed, I was so cozy." She confessed the last bit like it was a secret.

"I am glad you were comfortable, my . . ." Ah, I was

going to have to break this habit with her. "America."

I could tell she appreciated my effort. "Thank you." The smile faded from her face, and she fell into thought, absently chewing on her lip as she played with words in her head.

"I'm very sorry I was mean to you," she finally said. "I realized as I was trying to fall asleep that even though this is a strange situation for me, I shouldn't blame you. You're not the reason I got swept up in all this, and the whole Selection thing isn't even your idea." *Glad someone noticed.* "And then, when I was feeling miserable, you were nothing but nice to me, and I was, well, awful."

She shook her head at herself, and I noticed my heart seemed to be beating a bit faster.

"You could have thrown me out last night, and you didn't," she concluded. "Thank you."

I was moved by her gratitude, because I already knew she was past being anything close to insincere. Which brought me to a subject I had to broach if we were going to move forward. I leaned closer, elbows on my knees, both more casual and more intense than I'd been with the others already.

"America, you have been very up-front with me so far. That is a quality that I deeply admire, and I'm going to ask you to be kind enough to answer one question for me."

She gave a hesitant nod.

"You say you're here by mistake, so I'm assuming you don't want to be here. Is there any possibility of you having any sort of . . . of loving feelings toward me?"

It felt like she played with the ruffles on her dress for

hours while I waited for her to answer, and I sat there convincing myself that it was only because she didn't want to seem too eager.

"You are very kind, Your Majesty." *Yes.* "And attractive." *Yes!* "And thoughtful." *YES!*

I was grinning, looking like an idiot, I'm sure, so pleased she managed to see something positive in me after last night.

Her voice was low as she continued. "But for very valid reasons, I don't think I could."

For the first time, I was grateful Father trained me so well to hold myself together. I sounded quite reasonable when I questioned her. "Would you explain?"

She hesitated again. "I . . . I'm afraid my heart is elsewhere."

And then tears appeared in her eyes.

"Oh, please don't cry!" I begged in a hushed voice. "I never know what to do when women cry!"

She laughed at my shortcomings and dabbed at the corners of her eyes. I was happy to see her just so, lighthearted and genuine. Of course there was someone waiting for her. A girl this real would have to have been snatched up quick by some very smart young man. I couldn't imagine how she ended up here, but that really wasn't my concern.

All I knew was, even if she wasn't mine, I wanted to leave her with a smile.

"Would you like me to send you home to your love today?" I offered.

She gave me a smile that was more like a grimace. "That's

the thing . . . I don't want to go home."

"Really?" I leaned back, running my hand through my hair as she laughed at me again.

If she didn't want me, and she didn't want him, then what the hell *did* she want?

"Could I be perfectly honest with you?"

By all means. I nodded.

"I need to be here. My family needs me to be here. Even if you could let me stay for a week, that would be a blessing for them."

So she wasn't fighting for the crown, but I still had something she wanted. "You mean you need the money?"

"Yes." At least she had the decency to be ashamed of it. "And there are . . . certain people," she said with a meaningful look, "at home who I can't bear to see right now."

It took a second for it all to click. They weren't together anymore. She still cared about him, but she didn't belong to him. I nodded, seeing the predicament. If I could get away from the pressures of my world for a week, I would take it.

"If you would be willing to let me stay, even for a little while, I'd be willing to make a trade."

Now this was interesting. "A trade?" What in the world could she possibly offer?

She bit at her lip. "If you let me stay . . ." She sighed. "All right, well, look at you. You're the prince. You're busy all day, what with running the country and all, and you're supposed to narrow thirty-five, well, thirty-four girls, down to one? That's a lot to ask, don't you think?"

While it sounded like a joke, the truth was she cut to the core of my anxieties with absolute clarity. I nodded at her words.

"Wouldn't it be much better for you if you had someone on the inside? Someone to help? Like, you know, a friend?"

"A friend?"

"Yes. Let me stay, and I'll help you. I'll be your friend. You don't have to worry about pursuing me. You already know that I don't have feelings for you. But you can talk to me anytime you like, and I'll try and help. You said last night that you were looking for a confidante. Well, until you find one for good, I could be that person. If you want."

If I want . . . That wasn't an option, it seemed, but at least I could help this girl. And maybe enjoy her company a little bit longer. Of course, Father would be livid if he knew I was using one of the girls for such a purpose . . . which made me like it much, much more.

"I've met nearly every woman in this room, and I can't think of one who would make a better friend. I'd be glad to have you stay."

I watched as the tension melted from her body. Despite the knowledge that her affections were unattainable, I couldn't help but be drawn to try.

"Do you think that I could still call you 'my dear'?" I asked teasingly.

She whispered back, "Not a chance." Whether she meant it that way or not, it sounded like a challenge.

"I'll keep trying. I don't have it in me to give up."

She made a face, almost irked but not exactly. "Did you call all of them that?" she asked, jerking her head toward the rest of the girls.

"Yes, and they all seemed to like it," I replied, playfully smug.

The challenge in her smile was still there when she spoke. "That is the exact reason why I don't."

She stood, ending our interview, and I couldn't help but be amused by her again. None of the others were eager to cut our time together short. I gave her a small bow; she answered with a rather rough curtsy, and walked away.

I smiled to myself, thinking of America, measuring her against the other girls. She was pretty, if a bit rough around the edges. It was an uncommon type of beauty, and I could tell she wasn't aware of it. There was a certain . . . royal air she didn't seem to possess, though there was, perhaps, something regal in her pride. And, of course, she didn't desire me at all. Still, I couldn't shake the urge to pursue her.

And that was how the Selection did its first act in my favor: if I had her here, at least I had the chance to try.

Read on for an exclusive extended ending to

THE PRINCE

CHAPTER 7

"IF I HAVE ASKED YOU to remain behind, please stay in your seats. If not, please proceed with Silvia here into the dining hall. I will join you shortly."

I watched the girls cast glances at one another, some confused and others smug. I felt confident I'd made the right choices, and now came the task of dismissing them. It ought to be simple enough, especially since we'd hardly made contact. What would they be attached to?

The room emptied except for eight ladies, all smiling as they stood in front of me.

I stared back and suddenly wished that I had come up with some sort of speech before I lined them up.

"Thank you for staying a few extra minutes," I said, then stalled. "Um, I want to thank you for . . . for . . . coming to the palace and for giving me the opportunity to meet you."

Most giggled or lowered their eyes. Clarissa flipped her hair.

"I'm sorry to say, I don't think it's going to work out. Uh, you can go now?" The end sounded more like a question than a statement, and I was so grateful Father wasn't here to witness it.

One girl—Ashley, I think—immediately started crying, and I tensed.

"Is it because I dyed my hair?" the girl next to her said.

"Huh?"

"It's because I'm a Five, isn't it?" Hannah asked.

"You are?"

Clarissa ran up to me and clutched my hand. "I can be better, I swear!"

"What?"

Mercifully, a guard pulled her off me and escorted her from the room. I was left standing there, watching her go, completely stunned at the outpouring of emotion. They were meant to be ladies. What in the world was going on?

"But why?" one of the girls asked, so sweetly that it actually, physically pained me. It was Daphne all over again.

I missed who said it, but I turned to see them all wearing similar expressions of dejection, their hopes dashed, it seemed. We'd only met twenty minutes ago. How was this possible?

"I'm sorry," I said, truly feeling bad. "I just didn't feel anything."

Mia stepped forward, her face barely giving away that she

was on the edge of tears. Part of me admired her for her self-control. "What about how we feel? Doesn't that matter?"

She tilted her head, her brown eyes demanding an answer.

"Of course it does. . . ." *Maybe I should cave.* I didn't *have* to eliminate anyone the first day. But what kind of relationship would that create? I make a decision, she says I'm hasty, and then I give in?

No. This was my choice. I had to follow through.

"I'm very sorry to have caused you pain, but it's quite a challenge to cut thirty-five talented, charming, beautiful women down to one that I'm meant to marry." I spoke honestly, humbly. "I have to go with my gut. This is as much for the sake of your happiness as it is mine. I hope we can part from our short time together as friends."

Mia, unimpressed with my speech, gave me a cold glare before walking past me and out the doors. Nearly all of the girls followed her; it appeared we would not be leaving on good terms.

Ashley, who seemed the most upset, came up and quietly embraced me. I awkwardly put my arms around her, as she sort of pinned them down.

"I can't believe it's over so quickly. I really thought I had a chance." Her words came out in a stunned monotone. It sounded like she was talking to herself.

"I'm sorry," I repeated.

She stepped back, wiped her eyes, and once she was composed, gave me a very ladylike curtsy. "Good luck, Your Majesty."

She raised her head and walked away.

"Ashley," I called just before she reached the door.

She paused, hopeful.

No. I couldn't. I had to be firm.

"Good luck to you, too."

She smiled at me and left.

After a moment of silence, I looked to the guards in the room. "You can go," I ordered, desperate for a moment of privacy. I walked over to the couch I'd used to interview the girls and put my head in my hands.

You can only marry one of them anyway. It had to be done. Maybe it seemed hasty, but it wasn't. It was deliberate. You need to be deliberate.

I couldn't help doubting myself. Ashley had been sweet at the end. Had I already made a mistake? But I felt nothing when she sat in front of me, not even a tiny hint of a connection.

I drew in a breath and pulled myself up. It was done. Time to move forward. There were twenty-seven other girls I needed to focus on now.

Pasting a smile on, I walked across the wide hall into the dining room, where everyone was already eating. I noticed a few chairs begin to scoot back.

"Please don't rise, ladies. Enjoy your breakfasts." *Nothing is wrong. Everything is perfect.*

I kissed Mom on the cheek and gave Father a pat before sitting down myself, wanting to be the picture of the family the public expected us to be.

"A few gone already, Your Majesty?" Justin asked, pouring my coffee.

"You know, I once read a book about people who practiced polygamy. One man with several wives. Crazy. I was just in a room with eight very unhappy women, and I have no idea why anyone would choose that." My tone was light but the sentiment was real.

Justin laughed. "It's a good thing you only need one, sir."

"Indeed." I drank my coffee, taking it black, thinking of Justin's words.

I only needed one. Now, how did I find her?

"How many are gone?" Father asked, cutting his food.

"Eight."

He nodded. "Good start."

For all the doubt I felt, at least there was that.

I exhaled, trying to formulate a plan. I needed to get to know these girls individually. Scanning the room, I swallowed, considering the time and energy it was going to take to become close to twenty-seven girls.

A few of the Selected caught my wandering eyes and smiled as my gaze passed them. There were so many beautiful women here. I got the sense that a few of these girls had been on dates before and, perhaps foolishly, I was intimidated.

And then there was America, her mouth stuffed with a strawberry tart, her eyes rolling like she was in heaven. I stifled a laugh, and suddenly I had a plan.

"Lady America?" I called politely, nearly cracking up

again when she stopped chewing, eyes wide, as she turned to face me.

She covered her mouth with her hands, trying to finish quickly. "Yes, Your Majesty?"

"How are you enjoying the food?" I wondered if her mind went to last night when she admitted that was her main reason for staying. It was liberating somehow to tell a joke that only one person understood in front of a room of people.

Maybe I imagined the glint of mischief in her eye.

"It's excellent, Your Majesty. This strawberry tart . . . well, I have a sister who loves sweets more than I do. I think she'd cry if she tasted this. It's perfect."

I took a bite, needing a moment to orchestrate this. "Do you really think she would cry?" I asked.

America's lovely face squinted in thought. "Yes, actually, I do. She doesn't have much of a filter when it comes to her emotions."

"Would you wager money on it?" I shot back.

"If I had any to bet, I certainly would," she answered with a smile.

Perfect. "What would you be willing to barter instead? You seem to be very good at striking deals."

Father cut his eyes at me. That joke wasn't quite so well hidden.

"Well, what do you want?" she asked.

A first date that I can actually manage. A night with someone I don't have to try to impress because she claims it's impossible. A way to get this rolling again without making all of these girls hate me.

I smiled. "What do *you* want?"

She considered. Really, she could have asked for anything. I was prepared to bribe her if I had to.

"If she cries," she started hesitantly, "I want to wear pants for a week."

I pressed my lips together as the rest of the room laughed. Even Father was amused, or at least playing at it. But what I liked the best was that, while the room giggled at her request, she didn't duck her head or blush or think to ask for something else. She wanted what she wanted.

There was something charming about that.

"Done. And if she doesn't, you owe me a walk around the grounds tomorrow afternoon."

There were little sounds all over the room, including a sigh from Father at my choice. It was possible he was far more aware of the candidates than I was. She wouldn't be on his list of favorites. Hell, she wasn't really on the list at all.

America thought for a second and then nodded. "You drive a hard bargain, sir, but I accept."

"Justin? Go make a parcel of strawberry tarts and send it to the lady's family. Have someone wait while her sister tastes it, and let us know if she does, in fact, cry. I'm most curious about this." Justin gave me a quick nod and grin before heading on his way. "You should write a note to send with it, and tell your family you're safe. In fact, you all should. After breakfast, write a letter to your families, and we'll make sure they receive them today."

The girls—my girls—smiled joyfully. Over the course of the morning I'd met all the ladies, gotten most of their names right, dismissed several, and had arranged my first date. Though it left me feeling a little rattled, I'd have to call that a success.

"Sorry it took so long, Your Majesty. We had to go to a boutique in town," Seymour said, pulling a rack of pants on hangers behind him.

"Not a problem," I replied, setting aside the papers on my desk. I had decided to work in my room for the day. "What did you find?"

"We have several options, sir. I'm sure you'll find something for the lady here."

I stared at the clothes, absolutely confused. "So, what pants are good for women?"

Seymour shook his head and smiled. "Don't worry, Your Majesty, I've got this completely under control. Now, these white ones would look a bit more feminine and will go well with anything her maids make for tops. The same would be true for this pair."

He held out several options, and I tried to distinguish what made one better than the other, and guess at what she would like.

"Seymour, maybe this doesn't matter, but she's a Five. Do you think she'll feel comfortable in these?"

He looked at the rack. "If she's here, sir, she's likely seeking luxury."

"But if she was looking for luxury, would she have asked for pants in the first place?" I countered.

He nodded. "Jeans." Reaching toward the back of the rack he pulled out a pair of denim pants. I'd never actually worn jeans before. Didn't look particularly appealing. "I have a feeling these will be a winner."

I looked at my options again. "Yes, go with these, but throw that first pair you picked up in there as well. And maybe one more for good measure. Will these fit her?"

Seymour smiled. "We'll have them tailored and ready by this evening. Did the young lady win, then?"

I shrugged. "Not yet, but I'm hoping that if she does, and I give her more than she hoped for, she'll go on the date with me anyway."

"You must really like her," Seymour said, pushing the rack into the hallway.

I didn't answer, but as I shut the door, I thought about it. There was something about her. Even the way she didn't like me drew me in, and I couldn't help but smile.

CHAPTER 8

"Are you sure?" I asked.

"Absolutely," the courier said.

"Not a single tear?"

He grinned. "Not a one."

I paused outside America's door, unsure why my heart was beating so fast. She had no feelings for me; she'd made that quite clear. And that was my primary reason for choosing her first. This was going to be an easy date.

I expected a maid to answer the door, but when it rushed back, America was standing there, fighting a sarcastic smile.

"For the sake of appearances, would you please take my arm?" I asked, offering it to her. She sighed and took it, following me down the hall.

I'd expected her to start complaining, to say she really

should have won, but she was silent. Was she upset? Did she really not want to go with me?

"I'm sorry she didn't cry," I offered.

"No, you're not," she teased. With that, I knew she was fine. Maybe she was distracted somehow, but joking seemed to be our language. If we could find our way there, we'd be okay.

"I've never gambled before. It was nice to win."

"Beginner's luck," she shot back.

"Perhaps," I agreed. "Next time we'll try to make her laugh."

Her eyes went to the ceiling in thought, and I could guess where her mind was. "What's your family like?"

She made a face. "What do you mean?"

"Just that. Your family must be very different from mine." She had siblings, her house was small . . . people cried over pastries. I couldn't begin to imagine life in her family.

"I'd say so. For one, no one wears their tiaras to break-fast." She laughed, a musical sound, so fitting for a Five.

"More of a dinner thing at the Singer house?"

"Of course."

I couldn't help but chuckle. I liked her wit. It felt a bit similar to mine when she let it show. And it made me curi-ous if two people from two different worlds could grow up and be surprisingly the same.

"Well, I'm the middle child of five."

"Five!" Goodness, that must be loud.

"Yeah, five," she said, incredulous at my surprise. "Most

families out there have lots of kids. I'd have lots if I could."

"Oh, really?" Another similarity, and a very personal one.

Her bashful *yes* let me know it was an intimate detail for her as well. Maybe it shouldn't have felt awkward, but it did, discussing a future family with someone I was meant to have a chance with while knowing that I didn't.

"Anyway," she continued, "my oldest sister, Kenna, is married to a Four. She works in a factory now. My mom wants me to marry at least a Four." *What's wrong with a One?* "But I don't want to have to stop singing. I love it too much." *Oh, that makes sense. The guy at home must be a spectacular Five.*

"But I guess I'm a Three now," she continued, sounding sad. "That's really weird. I think I'm going to try to stay in music if I can. Kota is next. He's an artist. We don't see much of him these days. He did come to see me off, but that's about it."

There was something in her tone that hinted at pain or regret, but she moved on too quickly for me to ask about it.

"Then there's me," she said as we drew near to the stairs.

I beamed. "America Singer, my closest friend."

She playfully rolled her eyes, the blue in them catching the light. "That's right."

There was a strange comfort in those words.

"After me there's May. She's the one who sold me out and didn't cry. Honestly, I was robbed; I can't believe she didn't cry! But yeah, she's an artist. I . . . I adore her.

"And then Gerad. He's the baby; he's seven. He hasn't quite figured out if he's into music or art yet. Mostly he likes to play ball and study bugs, which is fine except that he can't make a living that way. We're trying to get him to experiment more. Anyway, that's everyone."

"What about your parents?" I asked, still trying to paint a full picture of her.

"What about your parents?" she countered.

"You know my parents."

"No, I don't. I know the public image of them. What are they really like?" she pleaded, pulling on my arm. Childish as it was, it made me smile.

But I was distracted. What could I possibly tell her about my parents?

I'm afraid my mother is sick. She has headaches a lot and seems tired. I can't tell if it's because of the way she grew up or if something happened later. I'm sure I'm supposed to have at least one sibling, and I can't tell if it's tied to that or not. My dad . . . Sometimes my dad . . .

We stepped into the garden and the cameras waited. Instantly, I felt on guard. I didn't want them here for this. I didn't know how far into the truth about myself or herself we might go, but I knew it wouldn't happen with an audience. After waving the crew away, I looked at America and realized she was distant again.

"Are you all right? You seem tense."

She shrugged. "You get confused by crying women, I get confused by walks with princes."

I smirked. "What about me is so confusing?"

"Your character. Your intentions. I'm not sure what to

expect out of this little stroll."

Was I so mysterious? Perhaps I was. I'd mastered smiles and half truths. But I certainly didn't want to appear that way.

I paused and turned to her. "Ah. I think you can tell by now that I'm not the type of man to beat around the bush. I'll tell you exactly what I want from you." *I want to know someone. Really know someone. And I think I want that person to be you, even if you leave.*

I stepped toward her and was suddenly stopped by a crippling pain. Yelling, I bent over and backed away. Those few steps were practically unbearable, but there was no way I was going to lie curled up on the ground, even though that was my instinct. I felt like I might vomit, and I fought that as well. Princes did not vomit and roll in the grass.

"What was that for?" Was that my voice? Really? I sounded like a five-year-old girl with a smoking problem.

"If you lay a single finger on me, I'll do worse!"

"What?"

"I said, if you—"

"No, no, you crazy girl. I heard you the first time. But just what in the world do you mean by it?"

She stood there wide-eyed again, covering her mouth as if she'd made a horrible mistake. I turned at the sound of the guard's footsteps and raised one arm while desperately holding myself with the other, dismissing them.

What had I done? What did she think I was . . . ?

I pulled myself together if only because I needed to know.

"What did you think I wanted?" I asked.

She lowered her eyes.

"America, what did you think I wanted?" I demanded.

Everything about her demeanor gave her away. I'd never been so insulted. "In public? You thought . . . for heaven's sake. I'm a gentleman!"

Though it was blindingly painful to do so, I stood a bit taller and walked away. Then something struck me.

"Why did you even offer to help if you think so little of me?"

She said nothing.

"You'll be taking dinner in your room tonight. I'll deal with this in the morning."

I moved as quickly as I could, eager to be away from her, hoping I might outrun the anger and humiliation. I slammed the door to my room, furious.

A second later, my butler knocked. "I heard you come in, Your Majesty. Can I get you anything before bed?"

"Ice," I whimpered.

He scurried away, and I fell into bed, consumed with rage. I covered my eyes, trying to process it all. I couldn't believe only minutes ago, I was about to open up to her, really share.

This was supposed to be my easy first date!

I huffed and heard my butler leave a tray on my bedside table and quickly exit.

Who did she think she was, a Five assaulting her future king? If I had the inclination, she could be seriously punished.

She was definitely going home. There was no way I would keep her here after that.

I stewed over the situation for hours, thinking of what I should have said or done in the moment. Every time I relived it, I was irate. What kind of girl did that? What made her think she could attack her prince?

I went over it a hundred times, but by the last time I thought it through, the irritation turned to some sort of awe.

Did America fear nothing?

Not that it was a theory I would test, but I wondered how many of the others, if placed in a situation where they thought I might take advantage of them, would allow it? For bragging rights, or maybe just because they worried what I would do if they didn't.

But she stopped it before it could even happen, not worried at all about what I might say. Even though she missed the mark completely, she stood up for herself. I genuinely admired that. It was a trait I wished I had myself. Maybe if I was around her enough, some of that would rub off on me.

Damn it. I had to let her stay.

THE GUARD

CHAPTER 1

"Wake up, Leger."

"Day off," I mumbled, pulling the blanket over my head.

"No one's off today. Get up, and I'll explain."

I sighed. I was normally excited to get to work. The routine, the discipline, the sense of accomplishment at the end of the day: I loved it all. Today was a different story.

Last night's Halloween party had been my last chance. When America and I had our one dance, and she explained Maxon's distance, I got a minute to remind her of who we were . . . and I felt it. Those threads that bound us together were still there. Perhaps they had frayed from the strain of the Selection, but they were holding.

"Tell me you'll wait for me," I'd pleaded.

She said nothing, but I didn't lose hope.

Not until he was there, marching up to her, dripping

charm and wealth and power. That was it. I'd lost.

Whatever Maxon had whispered to her out on the dance floor seemed to sweep every worry from her head. She clung to him, song after song, staring into his eyes the way she used to stare into mine.

So maybe I'd downed a little too much alcohol while I watched it happen. And maybe that vase in the foyer was broken because I threw it. And maybe I'd stifled my cries by biting my pillow so Avery wouldn't hear me.

If Avery's words this morning were any indication, chances were Maxon proposed late last night, and we would all be on call for the official announcement.

How was I supposed to face that moment? How was I supposed to stand there and *protect* it? He was going to give her a ring I could never afford, a life I could never provide . . . and I would hate him to my very last breath for it.

I sat up, keeping my eyes down. "What's happening?" I asked, my head throbbing with every syllable.

"It's bad. Really bad."

I scrunched my forehead and looked up. Avery was sitting on his bed, buttoning his shirt. Our eyes met, and I could see the worry in his.

"What do you mean? What's bad?" If this was some stupid drama over not finding the right colored tablecloths or something, I was going back to bed.

Avery exhaled. "You know Woodwork? Friendly guy, smiles a lot?"

"Yeah. We do rounds together sometimes. He's nice."

Woodwork had been a Seven, and we'd bonded almost instantly over our large families and deceased fathers. He was a hard worker, and it was clear that he was someone who truly deserved his new caste. "Why? What's going on?"

Avery seemed stunned. "He got caught last night with one of the Elite girls."

I froze. "What? How?"

"The cameras. Reporters were getting candid shots of people wandering around the palace and one of them heard something in a closet. Opened it up and found Woodwork with Lady Marlee."

"But that's"—I almost said *America's closest friend*, but caught myself just in time—"crazy," I finished.

"You're telling me." Avery picked up his socks and continued to dress. "He seemed so smart. Must have just had too much to drink."

He probably had, but I doubted that was why this had happened. Woodwork was smart. He wanted to take care of his family as much as I did mine. The only explanation for why he would have risked getting caught would be the same reason I had risked it: he must love Marlee desperately.

I massaged my temples, willing the headache to clear. I couldn't feel like this right now, not with something so big happening. My eyes popped open as I understood what this might mean.

"Are they . . . are they going to kill them?" I asked quietly, like maybe if I said it too loud everyone would remember that was what the palace did to traitors.

Avery shook his head, and I felt my heart start beating again. "They're going to cane them. And the other Elite and their families are going to be front and center for it. The blocks are already set up outside the palace walls, so we're all on standby. Get your uniform on."

He stood and walked to the door. "And get some coffee before you report in," he said over his shoulder. "You look like you're the one getting caned."

The third and fourth floors were high enough to see over the thick walls that protected the palace from the rest of the world, and I quickly made my way to a broad window on the fourth floor. I looked down at the seats for the royal family and the Elite, as well as the stage for Marlee and Woodwork. It seemed most of the guards and staff had the same idea I did, and I nodded at the two other guards who were standing at the window, and the one butler, his uniform looking freshly pressed but his face wrinkled with worry. Just as the palace doors opened, and the girls and their families went marching out to the thunderous cheering of the crowd, two maids came rushing up behind us. Recognizing Lucy and Mary, I made a space for them beside me.

"Is Anne coming?" I asked.

"No," Mary said. "She didn't think it was right when there was so much work to do."

I nodded. That sounded like her.

I ran into America's maids all the time since I guarded her door at night, and while I always tried to be professional in the palace, I tended to let some of the formality slip with them. I wanted to know the people who took care of my girl; in my eyes, I would forever be beholden to them for all the things they did for her.

I looked down at Lucy and could see she was wringing her hands. Even in my short time at the palace, I had noticed that when she got stressed, her anxieties manifested themselves in a dozen physical tics. Training camp taught me to look for nervous behavior when people entered the palace, to watch those people in particular. I knew Lucy was no threat, and when I saw her in distress, I felt a need to protect her.

"Are you sure you want to watch this?" I whispered to her. "It won't be pretty."

"I know. But I really liked Lady Marlee," she replied, just as quietly. "I feel like I should be here."

"She's not a lady anymore," I commented, sure that she would be torn down to the lowest rank possible.

Lucy thought for a moment. "Any girl who would risk her life for someone she loves certainly deserves to be called a lady."

I grinned. "Excellent point." I watched as her hands stilled and a tiny smile came to her face for a flicker of a second.

The crowd's cheers turned to cries of disdain as Marlee and Woodwork hobbled across the gravel and into the space cleared in front of the palace gates. The guards pulled them rather harshly, and based on his gait, I guessed Woodwork had already taken a beating.

We couldn't make out the words, but we watched as their crimes were announced to the world. I focused on America and her family. May looked like she was trying to hold herself in one piece, arms wrapped around her stomach protectively. Mr. Singer's expression was uneasy, but calm. Mer just seemed confused. I wished there was a way to hold her and tell her it was going to be all right without ending up bound to a block myself.

I remembered watching Jemmy being whipped for stealing. If I could have taken his place, I would have done it without question. At the same time, I remembered the overwhelming sense of relief that I had never been caught the few times I had stolen. I imagined America must be feeling that way right now, wishing Marlee didn't have to go through this, but so thankful it wasn't us.

When the canes came down, Mary and Lucy both jumped even though we couldn't hear anything but the crowd. There was just enough space between each lashing to allow Woodwork and Marlee to feel the pain, but not adjust to it before a new strike drove the burn in deeper. There's an art to making people suffer. The palace seemed to have it mastered.

Lucy covered her face with her hands and wept quietly while Mary put an arm around her for comfort.

I was about to do the same when a flash of red hair caught my eye.

What was she doing? Was she fighting that guard?

Everything in my body was at war. I wanted to run down there and shove her in her seat while at the same time, I was desperate to grab her hand and take her away. I wanted to cheer her on and simultaneously beg her to stop. This wasn't the time or place to draw attention to herself.

I watched as America hopped the rail, the hem of her dress flying in the fall. It was then, when she slammed into the ground and regrouped, that I saw she wasn't trying to take refuge from the nightmare in front of her but instead was focused on the steps it would take to get to Marlee.

Pride and fear swelled in my chest.

"Oh, my goodness!" Mary gasped.

"Sit down, my lady!" Lucy pleaded, pressing her hands against the window.

She was running, missing one shoe, but still refusing to give up.

"Sit down, Lady America!" one of the guards standing by me yelled.

She hit the bottom stair to the platform, and my brain was on fire from the pounding blood.

"There are cameras!" I shouted at her through the glass.

A guard finally caught her, knocking her to the ground. She thrashed, still putting up a fight. My gaze flickered to the royals; all their eyes were on the red-haired girl writhing on the ground.

"You should get back to her room," I told Mary and Lucy. "She's going to need you."

They turned and ran. "You two," I said to the guards. "Go downstairs and make sure extra protection isn't needed. No telling who caught that or might be upset by it."

They sprinted away, heading for the first floor. I wanted to be with America, to go to her room this very second. But under the circumstances, I knew patience would be the best. It was better for her to be alone with her maids.

Last night, I had asked America to wait for me, thinking she might be going home before me. Again, that idea came to the forefront of my mind. Would the king tolerate this?

I was aching all over, trying to breathe and think and process.

"Magnificent," the butler breathed. "Such bravery."

He backed away from the window and went back to his duties, and I was left wondering if he meant the couple on the platform or the girl in the dirty dress. As I stood there, still taking in all that had just happened, the caning came to an end. The royals exited, the crowd dispersed, and a handful of guards were left to carry away the two limp bodies that seemed to lean toward each other, even in unconsciousness.

CHAPTER 2

I REMEMBERED THE DAYS OF waiting to run to the tree house, how it seemed like the watch hands were moving backward. This was a thousand times worse. I *knew* something was wrong. I *knew* she needed me. And I couldn't get to her.

The best I could do was switch posts with the guard who was scheduled to watch her door tonight. Until night fell and I could see her again, I'd have to bury myself in my job.

I was heading to the kitchen for a late breakfast when I heard the complaints.

"I want to see my daughter." I recognized Mr. Singer's voice, but I'd never heard him sound so desperate.

"I'm sorry, sir. For safety reasons, we need to get you out of the palace now," a guard answered. Lodge, by the sound of it. I poked my head around the corner, and sure enough Lodge was there trying to calm Mr. Singer.

"But you've kept us caged since that disgusting display, my child was dragged away, and I haven't seen her! I want to see her!"

I approached them with an air of confidence and intervened. "Allow me to handle this, Officer Lodge."

Lodge dipped his head and stepped away. Most of the time, if I acted like I was in control, people listened to me. It was simple and effective.

Once Lodge was down the hall, I bent in toward Mr. Singer. "You can't talk like that here, sir. You saw what just happened, and that was over a kiss and an unzipped dress."

America's dad nodded and ran his fingers through his hair. "I know. I know you're right. I can't believe they made her watch that. I can't believe they did it to May."

"If it's any consolation, America's maids are very devoted, and I'm sure they're taking care of her. There was no report of her going to the hospital wing, so she must not have gotten hurt. Not physically anyway. From what I understand"— God, how I hated saying this out loud—"Prince Maxon favors her more than the others."

Mr. Singer gave me a thin smile that didn't quite meet his eyes. "True."

Everything in me fought against asking him what he knew. "I'm sure he'll be very patient with her as she deals with her loss."

He nodded then spoke under his breath, as if he was talking to himself. "I expected more from him."

"Sir?"

He took a deep breath and stood up straight. "Nothing." Mr. Singer looked around, and I couldn't tell if he was in awe of the palace or disgusted by it. "You know, Aspen, she'd never believe me if I told her she was good enough for this place. In a way she's right. She's too good for it."

"Shalom?" Mr. Singer and I both turned to see Mrs. Singer and May walking around the corner, carrying their bags. "We're ready. Have you seen America?"

May left her mother and quickly tucked herself into her father's side. He wrapped a protective arm around her. "No. But Aspen will check on her."

I hadn't said anything of that nature, but we were practically family and he knew that I would. Of course I would.

Mrs. Singer gave me a brief hug. "I can't tell you what a comfort it is to know you're here, Aspen. You're smarter than the rest of the guards combined."

"Don't let them hear you say that," I joked, and she smiled before pulling away.

May rushed over, and I bent down a little so we were on the same level. "Here are some extra hugs. Could you go by my house and give them to my family for me?"

She nodded into my shoulder. I waited for her to let go, but she didn't. Suddenly she pushed her lips to my ear. "Don't let anyone hurt her."

"Never."

She gripped me tighter, and I did the same, wanting so badly to protect her from everything around her.

May and America were bookends, alike in more ways

than either of them could see. But May was softer around the edges. No one sheltered her from the world; she sheltered herself. America had been only a few months older than May was now when we started dating, making a decision most people older than us would never have had the guts to face. But while America was aware of the bad around her, the consequences that could come if things ever went wrong, May practically skipped through life, completely blind to what was worst in the world.

I worried that some of that innocence had been stolen from her today.

She finally loosened her grip, and I stood, holding a hand out to Mr. Singer. He took it and spoke quietly. "I'm glad she has you. It's like she's got a piece of home with her."

My eyes locked on his, and again I was struck with the urge to ask him what he knew. I wondered if, at the very least, he suspected something. Mr. Singer's gaze was unwavering, and, because I'd been trained, I searched his face for secrets. I could never begin to guess at what he was hiding from me, but I knew without a doubt that there was something there.

"I'll look after her, sir."

He smiled. "I know you will. Look after yourself, too. Some would argue this post is even more dangerous than New Asia. We want you to come home safe."

I nodded. Out of the millions of words in the world, Mr. Singer always seemed to know how to pick the handful that made you feel like you mattered.

"I've never been treated so harshly," someone muttered, rounding the corner. "And at the palace of all places."

Our heads collectively turned. It sounded like Celeste's parents weren't taking the request to leave very well either. Her mother was dragging a large bag, shaking her head in agreement with her husband, flicking her blond hair over her shoulder every few seconds. Part of me wanted to walk over and hand her a pin.

"You there," Mr. Newsome said to me. "Come and fetch these bags." He dropped his suitcases on the floor.

Mr. Singer spoke up. "He's not your servant. He's here to protect you. You can carry your own bags."

Mr. Newsome rolled his eyes and turned to his wife. "Can't believe our baby has to associate with a Five." He whispered the words, though he obviously intended for all of us to hear.

"I hope she hasn't picked up any of her sloppy manners. Our girl's too good for that trash." Mrs. Newsome flicked her hair again, and I could see where Celeste learned to sharpen those claws of hers. Not that I expected anything more from a Two.

I could hardly look away from Mrs. Newsome's wickedly happy face, except for the muffled sound next to me. May was crying into her mother's shirt. As if this day hadn't been hard enough already.

"Safe trip, Mr. Singer," I whispered. He nodded to me and escorted his family through the front doors. I could see the cars were waiting already. America was going to hate that she didn't get to say good-bye.

I walked over to Mr. Newsome. "Don't let them bother you, sir. Leave your bags right here, and I'll make sure they're taken care of."

"Good lad," Mr. Newsome said, and patted me on the back before straightening his tie and pulling his wife along with him.

Once they were outside, I walked to the table near the entrance and pulled a pen out of the drawer. There was no chance of me getting away with doing this twice, so I had to decide which one of the Newsomes I hated more at the moment. Right now, it was Mrs. Newsome, if only for May's sake. I unzipped her bag, stuck the pen inside, and snapped it in half. I got a dot of ink on one hand, but seeing as I had thousands of dollars' worth of clothes in front of me to wipe it on, the mark was quickly taken care of. I watched as the Newsomes climbed into a car, then threw their bags into the trunk and allowed myself a small smile. But while destroying some of Mrs. Newsome's clothes was satisfying, I knew it wouldn't really affect her in the long run. She'd replace them within days. May would have to live with those words in her ears forever.

I held the bowl close to my chest as I lifted forkfuls of eggs and chopped sausage to my mouth, eager to get outdoors. The kitchen was packed with guards and servants, wolfing down meals as they started shifts.

"He was telling her he loved her through the entire thing,"

Fry was saying. "I was posted by the platform and could hear it the whole time. Even after she passed out, Woodwork was saying it."

Two maids hung on his every word, one tilting her head sadly. "How could the prince do that to them? They were in love."

"Prince Maxon is a good man. He was just obeying the law," the other maid shot back. "But . . . the whole time?"

Fry nodded.

The second maid shook her head. "No wonder Lady America ran for them."

I stepped around the large table, moving to the other side of the room.

"She kneed me pretty hard," Recen shared, wincing a little at the memory. "I couldn't stop her from jumping; I could barely breathe."

I smiled to myself, though I felt for the guy.

"That Lady America is pretty damn brave. The king could have put her on the block for something like that." A younger butler, wide-eyed and enthusiastic, seemed to be taking the whole thing in as entertainment.

I moved again, fearing I'd say or do something stupid if I heard any more. I passed Avery, but he only nodded. The set of his mouth and eyebrows was all I needed to see to know he wasn't interested in company right now.

"It could have been so much worse," a maid whispered.

Her companion nodded. "At least they're alive."

I couldn't escape it. A dozen conversations overlapped,

mixing into one commentary in my ears. America's name surrounded me, the word on nearly everyone's lips. I found myself swelling with pride one moment only to plunge into anger the next.

If Maxon truly was a decent man, America never would have been in this situation in the first place.

I took another swing with the ax, splitting the wood. The sun felt good on my bare chest and the act of destroying something was helping me get out my rage. Rage for Woodwork and Marlee and May and America. Rage for myself.

I lined up another piece and swung with a growl.

"Chopping wood or trying to scare the birds?" someone called.

I turned to see an older man a few yards away, walking a horse by the bit and wearing a vest that marked him as an outdoor palace worker. His face was wrinkled, but his age didn't dim his smile. I had a feeling that I'd seen him around before, but I couldn't think of the place.

"Sorry, did I spook the horse?" I asked.

"Nah," he said, walking over. "Just sounds like you're having a rough one."

"Well," I answered, lifting the ax again, "today has been rough on everyone." I swung, dividing the wood again.

"Yep. Seems to be the case." He rubbed the horse behind her ears. "Did you know him?"

I paused, not really sure I felt like talking. "Not well. We had a lot in common, though. I just can't believe it happened.

Can't believe he lost everything."

"Eh. Everything doesn't seem like anything when you love someone. Especially when you're young."

I studied the man. He was obviously a stable keeper, and though I could have been wrong, I was willing to guess he was younger than he looked. Maybe he'd been through something that had weathered him.

"You've got a point," I agreed. Wasn't I willing to lose everything for Mer?

"He'd risk it again. And so would she."

"So would I," I mumbled, staring at the ground.

"What, son?"

"Nothing." I shouldered the ax and grabbed another hunk of wood, hoping he'd take the hint.

Instead he leaned against the horse. "It's fine to be upset, but that won't get you anywhere. You gotta think about what you can learn from this. So far, looks like all you've learned is how to beat up on something that can't beat you back."

I swung and missed. "Look, I get that you're trying to help, but I'm working here."

"That ain't work. That's a whole lot of misplaced anger."

"Well, where am I supposed to place it? On the king's neck? On Prince Maxon's? On yours?" I swung again and hit. "Because it's not okay. They get away with everything."

"Who does?"

"They do. The Ones. The Twos."

"You're a Two."

I dropped the ax and yelled. "I'm a Six!" I hit my chest.

"Underneath whatever uniform they put on me, I'm still a kid from Carolina, and that's not going away."

He shook his head and pulled on the horse's bridle. "Sounds like you need a girl."

"I got a girl," I called at his back.

"Then let her in. You're swinging your fists for the wrong fight."

CHAPTER 3

I LET THE HOT WATER run over me, hoping the day would follow it down the drain. I kept thinking of the stable keeper's words, more angered by what he said than anything else that had happened.

I let America in. I knew what I was fighting for.

I toweled off, taking my time, trying to let the routine of getting dressed settle my mind. The starched uniform embraced my skin and with it came a sense of purpose and drive. I had work to do.

There was an order to things, and at the end of the day, Mer would be there.

I tried to stay focused as I walked to the king's office on the third floor. When I knocked, Lodge opened the door. We nodded at each other as I entered the room. I didn't always feel intimidated by the king, but within these walls I could watch as he changed thousands of lives with the flick of his finger.

"And we'll ban the cameras from the palace until further notice," King Clarkson said as an advisor took notes furiously. "I'm sure the girls have learned a lesson today, but tell Silvia to up the work on their decorum." He shook his head. "I can't begin to imagine what possessed that girl to do something so stupid. She was the favorite."

Maybe your *favorite,* I thought, crossing the room. His desk was wide and dark, and I quietly reached for the bin that held his outgoing mail.

"Also, make sure we keep an eye on that girl who ran."

My ears perked up, and I moved slower.

The advisor shook his head. "No one even noticed her, Your Majesty. Girls are such temperamental creatures; if anyone asked, you could just blame it on her erratic emotions."

The king paused, pushing back in his chair. "Perhaps. Even Amberly has her moments. Still, I never liked the Five. She was a throwaway, never should have made it this far."

His advisor nodded thoughtfully. "Why don't you simply send her home? Concoct a reason to eliminate her? Surely it could be done."

"Maxon would know. He watches those girls like a hawk. No matter," the king said, snapping back to his desk. "She's clearly not qualified, and sooner or later it will all surface. We'll get aggressive if we have to. Moving on, where was that letter from the Italians?"

I scooped up the mail and gave a quick unacknowledged

bow before leaving the room. I wasn't sure how to feel. I wanted America as far away from Maxon's hands as possible. But the way King Clarkson talked about the Selection made me think there was something more there, maybe something dark. Could America fall victim to one of his whims? And if America was a "throwaway," was she here by design? Brought specifically to be dismissed? If so, was there one girl who was expressly meant to be chosen? Was she still here?

At least I'd have something to think about while I stood outside America's door all night.

I thumbed through the mail, reading addresses as I walked.

In the small post room, three older men sorted the incoming and outgoing mail. There was one bin marked SELECTED that spilled over with letters from admirers. I wasn't sure how much of that the girls ever saw.

"Hey there, Leger. How you doing?" Charlie asked.

"Not great," I confessed, placing the mail in his hands, not risking it being lost in a pile.

"We've all seen better days, haven't we? At least they're alive."

"Did you hear about the girl who ran for them?" Mertin asked, spinning around in his chair. "Isn't that something?"

Cole turned, too. He was a pretty quiet guy, perfectly suited for the mail room, but even he was curious about this.

Nodding, I crossed my arms. "Yeah, I heard."

"What do you think?" Charlie asked.

I shrugged. It seemed that most people felt that America

had acted heroically, but I knew that if anyone said that in front of someone who devoutly adored King Clarkson, they might find themselves in serious trouble. For now, neutrality was best.

"The whole thing is a little crazy." I'd leave the perception of crazy good or crazy bad to him.

"Can't deny that," Mertin commented.

"Gotta get to my rounds," I said, ending the conversation. "See you tomorrow, Charlie." I gave him a little salute and he smiled.

"Stay safe."

I went down the hall to the storeroom to grab my staff, though I didn't see the purpose behind it. I preferred the gun.

As I rounded the stairs and landed on the second floor, I saw Celeste coming toward me. The moment she recognized my face, her whole demeanor shifted. It seemed that unlike her mother, she was at least capable of feeling shame.

She walked up to me cautiously, then stopped. "Officer."

"Miss." I bowed.

Her features looked sharp as she stood there, thinking over her words. "I just wanted to make sure that you knew the conversation we had last night was meant to be purely professional."

I nearly laughed in her face. Her hands might have stayed safely on my back and arms, but there was no mistaking the flirtation in her touch. She had been walking the line of breaking the rules herself. After I told her I had been a Six before becoming a guard, she suggested I look into modeling instead of staying in the service.

Her exact words had been, "If this doesn't work out for me, we're one and the same now. Look me up when you're out."

Celeste wasn't the kind of girl to wait around, so I didn't think she was truly attached to me in any way, and I suspected that her lips were especially loose last night because she'd had a little too much to drink. But there was one thing that was absolutely clear after our conversation: she didn't love Maxon. Not even close.

"Of course," I answered, knowing better.

"I simply wanted to give you career advice. Such a serious caste jump is hard to adjust to. And I wish you luck, but I want to be clear that my affections are singularly devoted to Prince Maxon."

I nearly called her on it. I was so close. But I saw the desperation in her eyes mixing with a consuming fear. In the end, if I accused her, I would accuse myself. I knew Maxon didn't matter to her, and I wasn't sure if any of these girls mattered to him—at least, not the way they should—but where would condemning her or playing some game get any of us?

"And I am wholly dedicated to protecting him. Good evening, miss."

I could see the lingering question in her eyes, and I knew she wasn't completely satisfied with my answer. But nothing could benefit a girl like that more than a little fear.

Inhaling, I rounded the corner to America's room, aching to walk in. I wanted to hold her, to talk to her. I stopped in front of the door and put my ear to it. I could hear her maids, so I knew she wasn't alone. But then I could make out her hitched breaths, the sniffs of her tired crying.

I couldn't handle the fact that she'd been crying all day. That was the last straw.

I'd promised her parents that Maxon favored her, and that she would be comforted. If she was still in tears, then he'd done nothing for her. If I wasn't meant to have her, he'd sure as hell better treat her like a princess. So far, he was failing catastrophically.

I knew—I *knew*—she was supposed to be mine.

I knocked on the door, not giving a damn about the consequences. Lucy answered, and she gave me a hopeful smile. That alone made me think I could be of help.

"I'm sorry to disturb you, ladies, but I heard the crying and wanted to make sure you were all right." I gently moved past Lucy, walking as close to America's bed as I dared. Our eyes locked, and she looked so helpless there, it was all I could do not to steal her away from this place.

"Lady America, I'm very sorry about your friend. I heard she was something special. If you need anything, I'm here."

She was silent, but I could see in her gaze that she was taking every tiny memory of our last two years and stringing them together with the future we'd always hoped to have.

"Thank you." Her voice was both timid and hopeful. "Your kindness means a great deal to me."

I gave her the smallest of smiles while inside my heart was thrashing. I'd studied her face in a dozen shades of light, in a thousand stolen moments. With her words, I knew without a doubt: she loved me.

CHAPTER 4

America loves me. America loves me. America loves me.

I had to get her alone, really alone. It would take some work, but I could make it happen.

Hours before my shift started the next morning, I was ready to go. I looked over all the guard posts, the cleaning rotations, the meal schedules for the royal family, the officers, and the help. I studied it until the lines overlapped in my head and I could see all the holes in the security. Sometimes I wondered if the other guards did this, too, or if I was the only one who looked close enough.

Either way, I had a plan. I just needed to get word to her.

My afternoon post was in the king's office, where I had the extraordinarily boring job of standing guard by the door. I liked being on the move, or at least in a more open part of the palace. Honestly, anywhere away from the cold gaze of King Clarkson.

I watched Maxon attempt to work. He looked distracted today, sitting at his small desk that seemed thrown in the room as an afterthought. I couldn't help but think that he was an idiot for being so careless with America.

Midmorning, Smiths, one of the guards who'd been at the palace for years, came rushing in. He darted over to the king, bowing quickly.

"Your Majesty, two of the Elite, Lady Newsome and Lady Singer, just got in a fight."

Everyone in the room paused, looking at the king.

He sighed. "Yelling like cats again?"

"No, sir. They're in the hospital wing. There was a little blood."

King Clarkson looked to Maxon. "No doubt that Five is responsible for this. You can't be serious about her."

Maxon stood. "Father, all of their nerves are frayed after yesterday. I'm certain they're having a difficult time processing the caning."

The king pointed a finger. "If she started it, she's gone. You know that."

"And if it was Celeste?" he countered.

"I doubt a girl of such high caliber would stoop so low without provocation."

"Still, would you dismiss her?" Maxon shot back.

"It wasn't her fault."

Maxon stood. "I'll get to the bottom of this. I'm sure it was nothing."

My mind was spinning. I didn't get him. He clearly wasn't treating America as well as he ought to, so why was he so determined to keep her? And if he failed to prove she wasn't at fault, would there be enough time for me to see her before she left?

The rumor mill at the palace was fast. In no time at all, I learned Celeste threw the first words, but Mer threw the first punch. I swear, I wanted to give my girl a medal. They were both staying—it seemed their actions canceled each other out—though it sounded like America was doing so begrudgingly.

Hearing those words made my heart even surer I'd gotten her back.

I ran to my room, trying to squeeze everything I needed to do into the few minutes I had. I scribbled the note as clearly and quickly as possible. Then I moved up to the second floor, waiting in a hallway until I saw America's maids leave to eat. When I got to her room, I debated over where to leave the letter, but there was really only one place to put it. I just hoped she'd see it.

As I made my way back into the main hallway, fate smiled on me. America didn't look like she was bleeding, so she must have left marks on Celeste. As she got closer, I could make out a small, swollen patch of skin almost completely covered by her hair. But past all that, I saw the excitement in her eyes the second she knew it was me.

God, I wished I could just sit with her. I breathed. Restraint now would mean real privacy later.

I stopped as we came close, bowing. "Jar."

I straightened and left, but I knew that she had heard. After a moment of thought, she nearly ran down the hall without a look back.

I smiled, happy to see the life come back to her. That was my girl.

"Dead?" the king asked. "By whose hand?"

"We're not sure, Your Majesty. But we could expect no less from down-casted sympathizers," his advisor said.

Walking in quietly to get the mail, I instantly knew he was talking about all the people in Bonita. Over three hundred families had recently been demoted at least a caste for their suspected support of the rebels. It seemed they weren't taking it without a fight.

King Clarkson shook his head before suddenly slamming his hand on the table. I jumped along with everyone else in the room.

"Don't these people see what they're doing? They're tearing apart everything we've worked for, and for what? To pursue interests they might fail in? I've offered them security. I've offered them *order*. And they rebel."

Of course the man with everything he could ever need or want didn't understand why any average person might want the same chance.

When I was drafted, I had been simultaneously terrified and thrilled. I knew that some considered it a death sentence.

But at least the life in front of me would be more exciting than the paperwork and housework I faced if I had stayed in Carolina. Besides, it wasn't much of a life anyway after America left.

King Clarkson stood, pacing. "These people have to be stopped. Who's running Bonita now?"

"Lamay. He's chosen to move his family to another location for the time being, and has started funeral arrangements for former Governor Sharpe. He seems to be proud of his new role, despite the obstacles."

The king held out his hand. "There. A man accepting his lot in life, doing his duty for the general public. Why can't they all do that?"

I scooped up the mail, close to the king as he spoke.

"We'll have Lamay eliminate any suspected assassins immediately. Even if he misses the mark, we'll send a clear warning. And let's find a way to reward anyone with information. We need to get some people in the South in our pocket."

I turned quickly, wishing I hadn't heard. I didn't support the rebels. More often than not, they were killers. But the king's actions today had nothing to do with justice.

"You there. Stop."

I looked back, not sure if the king was talking to me. He was, and I watched as he scrawled a brief letter, folded it, and added it to the pile.

"Take this with the post. The boys in the mail room will have the correct address." The king flung it onto the pile in my arms carelessly, like it held nothing of value. I stood there, immobile, unable to carry that load. "Go on," he finally said, and as always, I obeyed.

I took the pile and moved at a snail's pace toward the mail room.

This is none of your business, Aspen. You're here to protect the monarchy. This does that. Focus on America. Let the world go to hell around you so long as you can get to her.

I straightened and did what I must.

"Hey, Charlie."

He whistled as he took in the stack. "Busy day today."

"Looks like it. Um, there was this one . . . the king didn't have the address on hand, said you'd have it." I pointed to Lamay's letter on top.

Charlie flipped open the letter to see where it should go, scanning it quickly. By the end he looked troubled. He checked behind him before lifting his eyes to me. "Did you read this?" he asked quietly.

I shook my head. I swallowed, feeling guilty for not admitting that I already knew the contents. Maybe I could have stopped it, but I was only doing my job.

"Hmm," Charlie mumbled, quickly spinning in his chair and running into a stack of sorted mail.

"Come on, Charles!" Mertin complained. "That took me three hours!"

"Sorry about that. I'll tidy it up. Say, Leger, two things." Charlie picked up a lone envelope. "This came for you."

I immediately recognized Mom's handwriting. "Thank

you." I clung to the paper, desperate for news.

"Not a problem," he replied casually, picking up a wire basket. "And could you do me a favor and take this scrap paper for the furnace? Should probably go in right away."

"Sure thing."

Charlie nodded, and I tucked my letter away to get a better hold of the basket.

The furnaces were near the soldiers' quarters, and I set the basket down before carefully opening the door. The embers were low, so I tossed the papers in gingerly, leaving room for air to get to them.

If I hadn't needed to be so careful, I probably wouldn't have noticed the letter to Lamay stuck in with the empty envelopes and scraps of miswritten addresses.

Charlie, what were you thinking?

I stood there, debating. If I took it back, he would know he'd been caught. Did I want him to know he was caught? Did I want him to be caught at all?

I threw the letter in, watching to make sure it burned. I'd done my job, and the rest of the mail would go out. There would be no place to put blame, and who knew how many lives would be spared?

There'd been enough death, enough pain.

I walked away, washing my hands of it all. True justice would come eventually, to whomever was right or wrong in that situation. Because just now, it was hard to tell.

Back in my room, I tore into my letter, eager to hear from home. I didn't like Mom being without me. It was a small comfort that I could send her money, but I always worried for my family's safety.

It seemed the feeling was mutual.

I know you love her. But don't be stupid.

Of course she was two steps ahead of me, guessing things without prompting. She knew about America before I told her, knew how angry I was about things when I'd never said a word. And here she was, a country away, warning me to not do what she was positive I would.

I stared at paper. The king looked to be in the middle of a vicious streak, but I was sure I could keep out of his grasp. And my mother had never steered me wrong, but she didn't know how good I was at my job. I ripped the letter up and dropped it in the furnace on my way to meet America.

CHAPTER 5

I HAD TIMED IT PERFECTLY. If America made it within the next five minutes, no one would be aware of either of us. I knew what I was risking, but I couldn't stay away from her. I needed her.

The door creaked open then quickly shut. "Aspen?"

I'd heard her voice like that so often before. "Just like old times, eh?"

"Where are you?" I stepped from behind the curtain and heard her draw in a breath. "You startled me," she said playfully.

"Wouldn't be the first time, won't be the last."

America was many things, but stealthy wasn't one of them. As she tried to meet me in the middle of the room, she hit a sofa, two side tables, and tripped over the edge of a rug. I didn't want to make her nervous, but she really needed to be more careful.

"Shhh! The entire palace is going to know we're in here if you keep pushing things over," I whispered, more teasing than warning.

She giggled. "Sorry. Can't we turn on a light?"

"No." I moved into a more direct path for her. "If someone sees it shining under the door, we might get caught. This corridor isn't checked a lot, but I want to be smart."

She finally reached me, and everything in the world felt better the second I touched her skin. I held her for a second before ushering her to the corner.

"How did you even know about this room?"

I shrugged. "I'm a guard. And I'm very good at what I do. I know the entire grounds of the palace, inside and out. Every last pathway, all the hiding spots, and even most of the secret rooms. I also happen to know the rotations of the guards, which areas are usually the least checked, and the points in the day when the guards are at their fewest. If you ever want to sneak around the palace, I'm the guy to do it with."

In a single word, she was incredulous and proud. "Unbelievable."

I gave her a gentle tug, and she sat with me, the tiny scrap of moonlight barely making her visible. She smiled before turning serious.

"Are you sure this is safe?" I knew she was seeing

Woodwork's backside and Marlee's hands, thinking about the shame and loss that would be waiting if we were discovered. And that was if we were lucky. But I had faith in my skills.

"Trust me, Mer. An extraordinary number of things would have to happen for someone to find us here. We're safe."

The doubt didn't leave her eyes, but when I wrapped an arm around her, she fell into me, needing this moment as much as I did.

"How are you doing?" It was nice to finally ask.

Her sigh was so heavy it rattled me. "Okay, I guess. I've been sad a lot, and angry." She didn't seem to realize that her hand had instinctively gone to the patch of skin just above my knee, the exact place where she used to fiddle with the frayed hole on my jeans. "Mostly I wish I could undo the last two days and get Marlee back. Carter, too, and I didn't even know him."

"I did. He's a great guy." His family flitted through my mind, and I wondered how they were surviving without their main provider. "I heard he was telling Marlee he loved her the whole time and trying to help her get through it."

"He was. At least in the beginning anyway. I got hauled off before it was over."

I smiled and kissed the top her head. "Yeah, I heard about that, too." The second after I said it, I wondered why I didn't say that I *saw* it. I'd known what she did before the staff started whispering about it. But that seemed to be the way

I took it in: through everyone else's surprise and, usually, admiration. "I'm proud you went out with a fight. That's my girl."

She leaned in even closer. "My dad was proud, too. The queen said I shouldn't act that way, but she was glad I did. It's been confusing. Like it was almost a good idea but not really, and then it didn't fix anything anyway."

I held her tight, not wanting her to doubt what seemed natural to her. "It was good. It meant a lot to me."

"To you?"

It was awkward to admit my worries, but she had to know. "Yeah. Every once in a while I wonder if the Selection has changed you. You've been so taken care of, and everything is so fancy. I keep wondering if you're the same America. That let me know that you are, that they haven't gotten to you."

"Oh, they're getting to me all right, but not like that," she spat, her voice sharp. "Mostly this place reminds me that I wasn't born to do this."

Then her anger faded to sadness, and she turned toward me, burrowing her head into my chest, like if she tried hard enough she could hide under my ribs. I wanted to keep her in my arms, so close to my heart that she could practically be a part of it, and bat away all the pain that might come her way.

"Listen, Mer," I started, knowing the only way to get to the good would be to walk through the bad. "The thing about Maxon is that he's an actor. He's always putting on this perfect face, like he's so above everything. But he's just a person, and he's as messed up as anyone is. I know you cared about him or you wouldn't have stayed here. But you have to know now that it's not real."

She nodded, and I felt like this wasn't entirely new information to her, like a part of her always expected this.

"It's better you know now. What if you got married and then found out it was like this?"

"I know," she breathed. "I've been thinking about that myself."

I tried not to focus on the fact that she'd already wondered about a life married to Maxon. It was part of the experience. Sooner or later, she was bound to think about it. But that had passed.

"You've got a big heart, Mer. I know you can't just get over things, but it's okay to *want* to. That's all."

She was quiet, thinking over my words. "I feel so stupid."

"You're not stupid," I disagreed.

"I am, too."

I needed to make her smile. "Mer, do you think I'm smart?"

Her tone was light. "Of course."

"That's because I am. And I'm way too smart to be in love with a stupid girl. So you can drop that right now."

She gave a laugh like a whisper but it was enough to pierce through the sadness. I'd had my own aches because of the Selection, and I needed to try to understand hers better. She didn't ask to put her name in the lottery. I did. This was my fault.

A dozen times, I'd wanted to explain myself, to beg for the mercy that she'd already given. I didn't deserve it. Maybe now. Maybe this was the time that I could finally, really apologize.

"I feel like I've hurt you so much," she said, shame covering her voice. "I don't understand how you can still possibly be in love with me."

I sighed. She acted like she needed forgiveness, when it was certainly the other way around.

I didn't know how to explain this to her. There weren't words wide enough to hold what I felt for her. Not even I could make sense of it.

"It's just the way it is. The sky is blue, the sun is bright, and Aspen endlessly loves America. It's how the world was designed to be." I felt the lift of her cheek against my chest as she smiled. If I couldn't bring myself to apologize, maybe I could at least make it clear that those last minutes in the tree house were a fluke. "Seriously, Mer, you're the only girl I ever wanted. I couldn't imagine being with anyone else. I've been trying to prepare myself for that, just in case, and . . . I can't."

When the words failed, our bodies spoke. No kisses, nothing more than hushed embraces, but it was all we needed. I felt everything I had felt back in Carolina, and I was sure that we could be that again. Maybe be even more.

"We shouldn't stay much longer," I said, wishing it wasn't true. "I'm pretty confident in my abilities, but I don't want to push it."

She reluctantly stood, and I pulled her in for one last embrace, hoping it would be enough to sustain me until I could see her again. She held on tightly, like she was afraid to let me go. I knew the coming days would be hard for her, but whatever happened, I'd be here.

"I know it's hard to believe, but I'm really sorry Maxon turned out to be such a bad guy. I wanted you back, but I didn't want you to get hurt. Especially not like that."

"Thanks," she mumbled.

"I mean it."

"I know you do." She hesitated. "It's not over though. Not if I'm still here."

"Yeah, but I know you. You'll ride it out so your family gets money and you can see me, but he'd have to reverse time to fix this." I settled my chin on her head, keeping her as close to me for as long as I could. "Don't worry, Mer. I'll take care of you."

CHAPTER 6

I HAD A VAGUE SENSE that I was dreaming. America was across the room, tied to a throne, and Maxon had one hand on her shoulder, trying to push her into submission. Her worried eyes were locked on mine, and she struggled to get to me. But then I saw Maxon was watching me, too. His stare was menacing, and he looked so much like his father in that moment.

I knew I needed to get to her, to untie her so we could run. But I couldn't move. I was tied up, too, on the rack like Woodwork. Fear ran down my skin, cold and demanding. No matter how we tried we would never be able to save each other.

Maxon walked over to a pillow, picked up an elaborate crown, and brought it back to place on America's head. Though she eyed it warily, she didn't fight when he set it on her gleaming red hair. But it wouldn't stay put. It slipped over and over.

Undeterred, Maxon reached into his pocket and pulled out what looked like a two-pronged hook. He lined up the crown and pushed the hook in, affixing it to America's head. As the pin went in, I felt two massive stabs in my back and screamed from the burn of it. I waited to feel the blood, too, but it didn't come.

Instead, I watched as the blood spilled from the pins in America's head, mixing with the red of her hair and sticking to her skin. Maxon smiled as he shoved in pin after pin, and I yelled in pain every time one pierced America's skin, watching, horrified, as the blood from the crown drowned her.

I snapped awake. I hadn't had a nightmare like that in months, and never one about America. I wiped the sweat from my forehead, reminding myself that it wasn't real. Still, the pain from the hooks echoed on my skin, and I felt dizzy.

Instantly, my mind went to Woodwork and Marlee. In my dream, I would happily have taken all the pain if it meant America didn't have to suffer. Had Woodwork felt the same way? Had he wished he could have taken twice the punishment to spare Marlee?

"You all right, Leger?" Avery asked. The room was still dark, so he must have heard me tossing.

"Yeah. Sorry. Bad dream."

"It's cool. Not sleeping that great myself."

I rolled to face him even though I couldn't see a thing. Only senior officers had rooms with windows.

"What's going on?" I asked.

"I don't know. Would it be okay if I thought out loud for a minute?"

"Sure." Avery had been a great friend. The least I could do was spare him a few minutes of my sleep.

I heard him sit up, deliberating before he spoke. "I've been thinking about Woodwork and Marlee. And about Lady America."

"What about her?" I asked, sitting up myself.

"At first when I saw Lady America run for Marlee, I was pissed. Because shouldn't she know better? Woodwork and Marlee made a mistake, and they had to be punished. The king and Prince Maxon have to keep control, right?"

"Okay."

"But when the maids and butlers were talking about it, they were kind of praising Lady America. It didn't make sense to me because I thought what she did was wrong. But, well, they've been here a lot longer than we have. Maybe they've seen a lot more. Maybe they know something.

"And if they do, and they think Lady America was right to do what she did . . . then what am I missing?"

We were treading dangerous ground here. But he was my friend, the best I'd ever had. I trusted Avery with my life, and the palace was one place where I could really use an ally.

"That's a really good question. Makes you wonder."

"Exactly. Like sometimes when I'm on guard in the king's office, the prince will be working and then leave to do something. King Clarkson will pick up Prince Maxon's work and undo half of it. Why? Couldn't he at least talk to him about it? I thought he was training him."

"I don't know. Control?" As I said the word, I realized that had to be at least partially true. Sometimes I suspected Maxon didn't completely know what was going on. "Maybe Maxon isn't as competent as the king thinks he should be by now."

"What if the prince is *more* competent and the king doesn't like it?"

I held back the laugh. "Hard to believe. Maxon seems easily distracted."

"Hmm." Avery shifted in the dark. "Maybe you're right. It just seems like people feel differently about him than the king. And they talk about Lady America like if they could pick the princess, it would be her. If she's the type to disobey like that, does it mean that Prince Maxon would, too?"

His questions hit on things I didn't want to acknowledge. Could Maxon in fact be pushing against his father? And if that was the case, was he also pushing against the crown and all it stood for? I'd never been a fan of the monarchy; I didn't think I could seriously hate anyone who fought it.

But my love for America was bigger than everything else, and because Maxon stood between me and that love, I didn't think there was anything he could say or do that would make me consider him a decent person.

"I really don't know," I answered honestly. "He didn't stop what happened to Woodwork."

"Yeah, but that doesn't mean he liked it." Avery yawned.

"I'm just saying, we've been trained to watch every person who comes into the palace and to look for any hidden intentions. Maybe we should do the same with the people who are already here."

I smiled. "You might be on to something there," I admitted.

"Of course. I'm the brains of this whole operation." He rustled with his blankets, settling again.

"Go to sleep, brainiac. We'll need your smarts tomorrow," I teased.

"On it." He was still for maybe a whole minute before he piped up again. "Hey, thanks for listening."

"Anytime. What are friends for?"

"Yeah." He yawned again. "I miss Woodwork."

I sighed. "I know. I miss him, too."

CHAPTER 7

I DIDN'T MIND THE INJECTIONS so much, but they stung like hell for about an hour afterward. What was worse, they gave you this strange pulsing energy that lasted for most of the day. It wasn't uncommon to find a handful of guards running laps for hours or picking up some of the more laborious chores around the palace just to help burn it off. Doctor Ashlar made a point to limit the number of guards receiving them on any given day.

"Officer Leger," Doctor Ashlar called, and I went into the office and stood by the small examining table near his desk. The hospital wing was large enough to accommodate us, but this felt better done in private.

He nodded to acknowledge me, and I turned and pulled the waist of my pants down a few inches. I refused to allow myself to jump, not when the cold antiseptic swiped across my skin or when the needle pierced it.

"All done," he said cheerfully. "See Tom for your vitamins and compensation."

"Yes, sir. Thank you."

Every step throbbed, but I didn't let it show.

Tom gave me some pills and water, and after I downed them, I initialed his little paper and took my money, dropping it in my room before I headed out to the woodpile. Already, the urge to move was overwhelming.

Each swing of the ax brought a desperately needed release. I felt hypercharged today, fueled by the injections, Avery's questions, and that sinister dream.

I thought about the king saying that America was a throwaway. It seemed unlikely that America would win now when she was so upset with Maxon, but I wondered what would happen if the one person the king never intended to get the crown did?

And if Marlee had been a favorite, maybe even the king's personal pick to win, who was he pinning his hopes on now?

I tried to concentrate, but my thoughts blurred together under the insatiable drive to move. I swung and swung, and only stopped two hours later because there was nothing left to chop.

"There's a whole forest back there if you need some more."

I turned, and that old stable keeper was there, smiling.

"I think I might actually be done," I answered. As I got ahold of my breathing, I was sure the worst of the injection's effects had passed.

He walked closer. "You look better. Calmer."

I laughed, feeling the medicine evening out in my bloodstream. "It was a different energy I needed to burn off today."

He sat on the chopping block, looking completely at home. I had no idea what to make of this guy.

I rubbed my sweaty palms on my pants, trying to think of what to say. "Hey, I'm sorry about the other day. Didn't mean to give you a hard time, I—"

He held up his hands. "It's no problem. And I didn't mean to be pushy. But I've seen a lot of people let the bad around them make them hard or stubborn. In the end, they miss the chance to make their world better because they only see the worst in it."

There was still something about the tone of his voice and his features that made me feel like I knew him.

"I know what you mean." I shook my head. "I don't want to be like that. But I get so angry. Sometimes I feel like I know too much, or that I've done things I can't make right, and it just hovers over me. And when I see things happen that shouldn't . . . "

"You don't know what to do with yourself."

"Exactly."

He nodded. "Well, I'd start by thinking about what's good. Then I'd ask myself how I could make that good even better."

I laughed. "That doesn't make sense."

He stood. "You just think about it a bit."

As I walked back to the palace, I tried to figure out where

I might know him from. Maybe he'd passed through Carolina before he worked for the palace. Plenty of Sixes drifted. Wherever he'd been, whatever he'd seen, he hadn't let it bring him down. I should have asked for his name, but we seemed to be running into each other a lot, so I figured we'd meet again soon. When I wasn't in an awful mood, he was actually a pretty decent guy.

After cleaning up, I made my way to my room, still thinking about the stable keeper's words. What was good? How could I make it better?

I picked up the envelope with my money in it. I didn't need to use a cent of it at the palace, so all of it went to my family. Usually.

I scribbled a note to Mom.

SORRY it's NOT AS much this time. SOMETHING CAME UP. MORE NEXT WEEK. LOVE you, ASPEN.

Shoving a little less than half of my earnings in an envelope with the letter, I pushed it aside and pulled out another piece of paper.

I knew Woodwork's address by heart, seeing as I'd written it out for him a dozen times. Illiteracy seemed more common than most people knew, but Woodwork was so worried about people thinking he was stupid or worthless that I was the only guard he'd trusted with his secret.

Depending on lots of things—where you lived, how large

your school was, if it was more Seven heavy—a person might make it through a decade of instruction and know next to nothing.

I couldn't say Woodwork slipped through the cracks. He was pushed into a gaping hole.

And now, we had no idea where he was, how he was doing, or if Marlee was even still there for him.

> Mrs. Woodwork,
> It's Aspen. We're all sorry about your son. I hope you're doing okay. This was the last of his compensation. Just wanted to make sure you got it. Take care.

I debated saying more. I didn't want her to think she was getting charity, so brevity seemed best. But maybe from time to time, I could send her something anonymously.

Family was good, and Woodwork's was still around. I had to try and help them.

CHAPTER 8

I WAITED UNTIL I WAS sure everyone was asleep before I opened America's door. I was thrilled to find her still awake. I'd been wishing she'd wait up for me, and the way she sort of tilted her head and shifted closer made me think she'd hoped I'd be here tonight.

I left the door open as always and bent down by her bed. "How have you been?"

"All right, I suppose." But I could tell she didn't mean that. "Celeste showed me this article today. I'm not sure I want to get into it. I'm so tired of her."

What was it with that girl? Did she think she could torture people and manipulate her way to a crown? Her continued presence here was one more example of Maxon's horrible taste.

"I guess with Marlee gone, he won't be sending anyone home for a while, huh?"

It looked like it took all of her energy to muster up a sad little shrug.

"Hey." I moved a hand to her knee. "It's going to be all right."

She gave me a weak smile. "I know. I just miss her. And I'm confused."

"Confused about what?" I asked, moving to a more comfortable position to listen.

"Everything." Her voice was so desperate. "What I'm doing here, who I am. I thought I knew." She fidgeted her hands, like maybe she could catch the right words. "I don't even know how to explain it right."

I looked at America and realized that losing Marlee and finding out the truth about Maxon's character had exposed her to truths she didn't want to think were out there. It sobered her up—maybe too quickly. She seemed paralyzed now, afraid of taking any kind of step because she didn't know what would fall apart along the way. America had seen me lose my father and deal with Jemmy's beating, and she'd watched as I struggled to keep my family fed and safe. But she'd only *seen* that; she hadn't experienced it. Her family was intact, save her loser brother, and she'd never really lost anything.

Except maybe you, you idiot, a part of me accused. I shook the thought away. This moment was about her, not me.

"You know who you are, Mer. Don't let them try to change you."

She twitched her hand, like she might reach down and touch mine. She didn't, though.

"Aspen, can I ask you something?" Concern still painted every corner of her face.

I nodded.

"This is kind of strange, but if being the princess didn't mean I had to marry someone, if it was just a job someone could pick me for, do you think I could do it?"

Whatever I had been expecting, that wasn't it. I had a hard time believing she was even still considering becoming the princess. Then again, maybe she wasn't. This was hypothetical, and she'd said to think about it without her being linked to Maxon.

Considering the way she'd handled everything that had happened publicly, I could guess she'd feel helpless when confronted with the things that happened behind closed doors. She was great at a lot of things, but . . .

"Sorry, Mer. I don't. You don't have it in you to be as calculating as they are." I tried to convey that I wasn't insulting her. If anything, I was happy she wasn't that person.

She furrowed her thin eyebrows. "Calculating? How so?"

I exhaled, trying to think of how to explain this without being too specific. "I'm everywhere, Mer. I hear things. There's a lot of turmoil down South, in the areas with a heavy concentration of lower castes. From what the older guards say, those people never particularly agreed with Gregory Illéa's methods, and there's been unrest down there for a long time. Rumor has it, that was part of why the queen was so attractive to the king. She came from the South, and it appeased them for a while. Not so much anymore it seems."

She considered this. "That doesn't explain what you meant by calculating."

How bad could it be if I shared what I knew with her? She kept our relationship a secret for two years. I could trust her. "I was in one of the offices the other day, before all the Halloween stuff. They were mentioning rebel sympathizers in the South. I was told to see these letters to the postal wing safely. It was over three hundred letters, America. Three hundred families who were getting knocked down a caste for not reporting things or for helping someone the palace saw as a threat."

She inhaled sharply, and I watched as dozens of scenarios unfolded in front of her eyes.

"I know. Can you imagine? What if it was you, and all you knew how to do was play the piano? Suddenly you're supposed to know how to do clerical work, how to find those jobs even? It's a pretty clear message."

Her concern shifted. "Do you . . . Does Maxon know?"

That was a good question. "I think he has to. He's not that far off from running the country himself."

She nodded and let that settle in on top of all the other new things she had learned about her sort-of boyfriend.

"Don't tell anyone, okay?" I pleaded. "A slip like that

could cost me my job." *And so much more,* I added in my head.

"Of course. It's already forgotten." Her tone was light, trying to mask the weight of her worries. Her efforts made me smile.

"I miss being with you, away from all this. I miss our old problems," I lamented. What wouldn't I give to be irritated about her making me dinner now?

"I know what you mean," she said with a giggle. A real one. "Sneaking out of my window was so much better than sneaking around a palace."

"And scrounging to find a penny for you was better than having nothing to give you at all." I tapped on the jar by her bed. I always took that as a good sign, that she kept it nearby before I was even in the palace. "I had no idea you'd saved them all until the day before you left," I added, remembering in awe the weight of them being poured into my palms.

"Of course I did!" she exclaimed proudly. "When you were away, they were all I had to hold on to. Sometimes I used to pour them over my hand on the bed, just to scoop them up again. It was nice to have something you touched."

She was as bad as I was. I never took anything from her to keep as my own, but I stored up every moment like it was a physical thing. I'd thumb through memories whenever things were still. I spent more time with her than she ever knew.

"What did you do with all of them?" she wondered.

I smiled. "They're at home, waiting." I'd had a small store of money to marry America saved up before she left. These days I had my mom set aside a portion of each paycheck for me, and I was sure she knew what I was putting it toward. But my most precious corner of that stash was the pennies.

"For what?"

For a decent wedding. For actual rings. For a home of our own. "That, I cannot say."

I'd tell her everything soon enough. We were still working our way back to each other.

"Fine, keep your secrets," she said, pretending to be annoyed. "And don't worry about not giving me anything. I'm just happy you're here, that you and I can at least fix things, even if it's not what it used to be."

I frowned. Were we that far from what we once were? So far that she needed to address it? No. Not to me. We were still those people back in Carolina, and I needed her to remember that.

I wanted to give her the world, but all I had at the moment were the clothes on my back. I looked down, plucked off a button, and held it up to her.

"I literally have nothing else to give you, but you can hold on to this—something I've touched—and think of me anytime. And you can know that I'm thinking of you, too."

She took the tiny, golden button from my hand, and stared at it like I'd given her the moon. Her lip trembled and she breathed slowly, as if she might cry. Maybe I'd done this all wrong.

"I don't know how to do this right now," she confessed. "I feel like I don't know how to do anything. I . . . I haven't forgotten you, okay? It's still here."

She put her hand on her chest, and I saw her fingers dig into her skin, trying to calm whatever was happening inside.

Yes, we still had a long way to go, but I knew it wouldn't feel that way if we were in it together.

I smiled, needing nothing more. "That's enough for me."

CHAPTER 9

I'D HEARD ABOUT THE KING'S tea party for the ladies of the Elite and knew America wouldn't be in her room when I came knocking.

"Officer Leger," Anne said, opening the door with a wide smile. "What a pleasure to see you."

At her words, Lucy and Mary walked over to greet me.

"Hello, Officer Leger," Mary said.

"Lady America is out right now. Tea with the royal family," Lucy added.

"Oh, I know. I was wondering if I could chat with you ladies for a moment."

Anne gestured for me to come in. "Of course."

I made my way to the table, and they hurried to pull out a chair for me. "No," I insisted, "you sit."

Mary and Lucy took the two seats, while Anne and I stood.

I took off my hat and rested a hand on the back of Mary's chair. I wanted them to feel comfortable talking with me, and I hoped dropping a little of the formality would allow for that.

"How can we help you?" Lucy asked.

"I was just doing a security sweep, and I wanted to see if you've noticed anything unusual. Probably sounds silly, but the littlest things can help us keep the Elite safe." There was truth to that, but we weren't exactly charged with seeking out that information.

Anne bowed her head in thought while Lucy's eyes went to the ceiling as she wondered.

"I don't think so," Mary started.

"If anything, Lady America has been less active since Halloween," Anne offered.

"Because of Marlee?" I guessed. They all nodded in answer.

"I'm not sure she's over it," Lucy said. "Not that I blame her."

Anne patted her shoulder. "Of course not."

"So, beyond her trips to the Women's Room and meals, she's more or less staying in her room?"

"Yes," Mary confirmed. "Lady America has done that in the past, but these last few days . . . it's like she just wants to hide."

From that, I deduced two important things. First, America wasn't spending time alone with Maxon anymore. Second, our meetings were still going undetected, even by those closest to her.

Both of those details caused the hope in my heart to swell.

"Is there anything else we should be doing?" Anne asked. I smiled because it was the kind of question I would have asked if I were her, trying to figure out how to get ahead of a problem.

"I don't think so. Pay attention to things you're seeing and hearing, as always, and feel free to contact me directly if you think anything is off."

Their faces were all eager, so ready to please.

"You're a wonderful soldier, Officer Leger," Anne said.

I shook my head. "Just doing my job. And, as you know, Lady America is from my province, and I want to look out for her."

Mary turned to me. "I think it's so funny that you're from the same province and you're basically her personal guard now. Did you live near her in Carolina?"

"Sort of." I tried to keep our closeness vague.

Lucy smiled brightly. "Did you ever see her when she was younger? What was she like growing up?"

I couldn't help but grin. "I ran across her a few times. She was a tomboy. Always outside with her brother. Stubborn as a mule, and as I remember, very, very talented."

Lucy giggled. "So basically the same as ever," she said, and they all laughed.

"Pretty much," I confirmed.

Those words made the feeling in my chest grow even more. America was a thousand familiar things, and beneath the ball gowns and jewelry, they were all still there.

"I should get downstairs. I want to make sure to catch the *Report*." I reached across the girls to pick up my hat.

"Maybe we should come with you," Mary suggested. "It's almost time."

"Certainly." For the staff, the *Report* was the one time television was permitted, and there were only three places to watch: the kitchen, the workroom where the maids did their sewing, and a large common room that generally turned into another workspace instead of a place to commune. I preferred the kitchen. Anne led the way there, while Mary and Lucy stayed back with me.

"I did hear something about visitors, Officer Leger," Anne said, pausing for a moment to share. "But that might only be a rumor."

"No, it's true," I answered. "I don't know any details, but I hear we have two different parties coming."

"Yay," Mary said sarcastically, "I know I'm gonna get stuck with tablecloth steaming again. Hey, Anne, whatever you get assigned with, can we trade?" she asked, scurrying up to Anne as they got in a debate over their yet-to-be-determined tasks.

I held out my arm for Lucy. "Madam."

She smiled and looped her hand through, sticking her nose in the air. "Good sir."

We moved down the hallway. As they chatted about errands that needed to be done and dresses that needed hemming, I realized why I was almost always happiest when I spent time with America's maids.

I could be a Six with them.

I sat on a counter with Lucy on one side and Mary on the other. Anne hovered, shushing people as the *Report* began.

Each time the cameras got a shot of the girls, I could tell something was wrong. America looked dejected. What was worse, I could tell she was trying not to look that way and failing spectacularly.

What was she so worried about?

Out of the corner of my eye, I saw Lucy wringing her hands.

"What's wrong?" I whispered.

"Something isn't right with my lady. I can see it in her face." Lucy pulled one hand up to her mouth and started chewing away on a nail. "What's happened to her? Lady Celeste looks like a cat on the prowl. What will we do if she wins?"

I put my hand on the one in her lap, and miraculously, she stilled, looking bewilderedly into my eyes. I got the feeling that people ignored Lucy's nerves.

"Lady America will be fine."

She nodded, comforted by the words. "But I like her," she whispered. "I want her to stay. It seems like everyone leaves when I need them to stay."

So Lucy had lost somebody. Maybe a lot of somebodies.

I felt like I understood her anxiety problems a little better.

"Well, you're stuck with me for four years." I gently elbowed her and she smiled, holding the tears in her eyes at bay.

"You're so nice, Officer Leger. We all think so." She dabbed at her lashes.

"Well, I think you ladies are nice, too. I'm always happy to see you."

"We're not ladies," she answered, looking down.

I shook my head. "If Marlee can still be a lady because she sacrificed herself for someone who mattered to her, then you certainly can. The way I see it, you sacrifice your life every day. You give your time and energy to someone else, and that's the exact same thing."

I saw Mary peek over before focusing on the television again. Anne might have noticed my words as well. She looked like she was leaning in to hear.

"You're the best one we have, Officer Leger."

I smiled. "When we're down here, you three can call me Aspen."

CHAPTER 10

STARING AT THE WALL LOST its excitement about thirty minutes in to standing watch. It was well past midnight now, and all I could do was count the hours until sunrise. But at least my boredom meant that America was safe.

The day had been uneventful except for the final confirmation of the coming visitors.

Women. So many women.

Part of me felt encouraged by that news. The ladies who came to the palace tended to be less aggressive physically. But their words could probably start wars if said in the wrong tone.

The members of the German Federation were old friends, so we had that working in our favor securitywise. The Italians were wild cards.

I'd thought of America all night, wondering what her

appearance on the *Report* meant. I wasn't sure I wanted to question her about it, though. I'd leave it to her. If she got the chance to share, I'd listen. For now, she needed to focus on what was coming. The longer she stayed at the palace, the longer I had her with me.

I rolled my shoulders, listening to my bones pop. Just a few more hours to go. I straightened and caught a set of blue eyes peeking around the edge of the hallway. "Lucy?"

"Hello," she answered, coming around the corner. Just behind her, Mary followed holding a small basket in her arm, the contents wrapped with cloth.

"Did Lady America ring for you? Is everything all right?" I reached for the handle to open the door for them.

Lucy put a delicate hand on her chest, seeming nervous. "Oh, everything's fine. Um, we were coming to see if you were here."

I squinted, moving my hand back. "Well, I am. Do you need something?"

They looked at each other before Mary spoke up. "We just noticed you've been working a lot of shifts the last few days. We thought you might be hungry."

Mary pulled back the cloth, revealing a small assortment of muffins, pastries, and bread, probably overspill from breakfast preparations.

I gave a half smile. "That's very nice of you, but, one, I'm not supposed to eat while I'm on duty, and, two, you might have noticed that I'm a pretty strong guy." I flexed my free arm and they giggled. "I can take care of myself."

Lucy tilted her head. "We know you're strong, but accepting help is its own kind of strength."

Her words nearly took the breath out of me. I wished someone had told me that months ago. I could have saved myself so much grief.

I looked at their faces, so much like America's that last night in the tree house: hopeful, excited, warm. My eyes moved to the basket of food. Was I really going to keep doing this? Alienating the few people who genuinely made me feel like myself?

"Here's the deal: if anyone comes, you wrestled me to the ground and forced me to eat. Got it?"

Mary grinned, holding out the basket. "Got it."

I took a piece of cinnamon bread and bit it. "You're gonna eat, too, right?" I asked as I chewed.

Lucy clasped her hands together enthusiastically before hunting through the basket, and Mary quickly followed suit.

"So, how good are your wrestling skills?" I joked. "I mean, I want to make sure we've got our story straight."

Lucy covered her mouth, giggling. "Funny enough, that's not part of our training."

I gasped. "What? This is important stuff here. Cleaning, serving, hand-to-hand combat."

They chuckled as they ate.

"I'm serious. Who's in charge? I'm going to write a letter."

"We'll mention it to the head maid in the morning," Mary promised.

"Good." I took a bite and shook my head in mock outrage.

Mary swallowed. "You're so funny, Officer Leger."

"Aspen."

She smiled again. "Aspen. Are you going to stay when your term is up? I'm sure if you applied, the palace would want you as a permanent guard."

Now that I was a Two, I knew I wanted to keep being a soldier . . . but at the palace?

"I don't think so. My family is back in Carolina, so I'll probably try to serve there if I can."

"That's a shame," Lucy whispered.

"Don't get sad just yet. I still have four years to go."

She gave a tiny smile. "True."

But I could tell she hadn't really shaken it off. I remembered Lucy mentioning earlier that people she cared about tended to leave, and it felt bittersweet that somehow I'd become important to her. She mattered to me, too, of course. So did Anne and Mary. But their connection to me was almost exclusively through America. How had I become significant to them?

"Do you have a big family?" Lucy asked.

I nodded. "Three brothers: Reed, Becken, and Jemmy, and three sisters: Kamber and Celia, who are twins, and then Ivy is the youngest. Plus my mom."

Mary started covering the basket again. "What about your dad?"

"He died a few years ago." I'd finally gotten to a place where I could say that without it tearing me apart. It used to feel crippling, because I still needed him. We all did. But I was lucky. Sometimes fathers would simply disappear in the lower castes, leaving those behind to fend for themselves or sink.

But my dad did everything he could for us, right up until the end. Because we were Sixes, things would always be hard, but he kept us above a line, let us maintain some pride in what we did and who we were. I wanted to be like that.

The paychecks would be nicer at the palace, but I could do a better job of providing if I was at least closer to home.

"I'm sorry," Lucy said softly. "My mom died a few years ago, too."

Knowing Lucy lost the most important person in her life reframed her in my mind, pulling everything together.

"Never quite the same, is it?"

She shook her head, eyes focused on the carpet. "But still, we have to look for the good."

Her face came up, and there was the faintest whisper of hope in her expression. I couldn't help but stare.

"It's so funny that you said that."

She looked to Mary and back to me. "Why?"

I shrugged. "Just is." I popped the last bite of bread in my mouth and wiped a few crumbs off my fingers. "Thank you, ladies, for the food, but you should go. It's not exactly safe to be running around the palace at night."

"Okay," Mary said. "We should probably start working on those wrestling skills anyway."

"Go jump on Anne," I advised her. "Never underestimate the element of surprise."

She laughed again. "We won't. Good night, Officer Leger." She turned to walk down the hall.

"Hold on," I urged, and they both stopped. I nodded toward the wall that held a secret passage. "Would you take the back way? It'd make me feel a lot better."

They smiled. "Of course."

Mary and Lucy waved as they passed, but when they got to the wall and Mary pushed it open, Lucy whispered something to her. Mary nodded and scurried downstairs, but Lucy came back to me.

She fidgeted with her hands, those little tics surfacing again as she approached.

"I'm not . . . I'm not good at saying things," she admitted, rocking a bit on her feet. "But I wanted to thank you for being so nice to us."

I shook my head. "It's nothing."

"Not to us, it isn't." There was an intensity in her eyes I'd never seen before. "No matter how many times the laundry maids or the kitchen maids tell us we're lucky, it doesn't really feel that way unless someone appreciates you. Lady America does, and none of us were expecting that. But you do it, too.

"You're both kind without even thinking about it." She smiled to herself. "I just thought you should know it was significant. Maybe to Anne more than anyone, but she'd never say it."

I didn't know how to respond. After struggling for a moment, the only thing that came out was, "Thank you."

Lucy nodded and, not sure what else to say, headed for the passage.

"Good night, Miss Lucy."

She turned back, looking like I'd given her the best present in the world. "Good night, Aspen."

When she left, my thoughts turned back to America. She'd looked so upset today, but I wondered if she had any idea how her attitude changed the people around her. Her dad was right: she was too good for this place.

I'd have to find a time to tell her how she was helping people without even knowing it. For now, I hoped she was resting, unworried about whatever had—

I whipped my head, watching as three butlers ran past, one tripping a bit as he moved. I was walking to the edge of the hall to see what they were running from when the siren sounded.

I'd never heard it before tonight, but I knew what that sound meant: rebels.

I sprinted back and burst into America's room. If people were running, maybe we were already behind.

"Damn it, damn it, damn it," I muttered. She needed to get dressed fast.

"Huh?" she said sleepily.

Clothes. I needed to find clothes. "Get up, Mer! Where are your damn shoes?"

She flicked her blanket off and stepped right into them. "Here. I need my robe," she added, pointing as she adjusted her shoes. I was glad she understood the urgency so quickly.

I found the bundled fabric at the end of her bed and tried to make heads or tails of it.

"Don't bother, I'll carry it." She pulled it out of my hands, and I rushed her to the door.

"You need to hurry," I warned. "I don't know how close they are."

She nodded. I could feel the adrenaline pulsing through me, and though I knew better, I jerked her back, embracing her in the dark.

I pushed my lips to hers, locking her to me with a hand knotted into her hair. Stupid. So, so stupid. But right in a thousand ways. It felt like an eternity had passed since we'd kissed this deeply, but we fell into it so easily. Her lips were warm, and the familiar taste of her skin lingered in them. Underneath the faintest hint of vanilla, I could smell her, too, the natural scent that clung to her hair and cheeks and neck.

I would have stayed there all night, and sensed she might have done the same, but I needed her to get to the safe room.

"Go. Now," I ordered, pushing her into the hallway, not looking back as I rounded the corner to face whatever was waiting for me.

I unholstered my gun, checking in both directions for anything out of place. I saw the swish of a maid's skirt as she ducked into one of the secret safe rooms. I hoped that Lucy and Mary had already made their way to Anne and were hidden in their quarters, far away from danger.

Hearing the unmistakable sound of shots being fired, I

ran down the hall toward the main stairwell. It sounded like the rebels were contained to the first floor, at least, so I knelt at the corner of the wall, watching the curve of the steps, waiting.

A moment later, someone ran up the stairs. It took less than a second for me to identify the man as an intruder. I aimed and fired, hitting him in the arm. With a grunt the rebel fell back, and I saw a guard bolting up to capture him.

A crash down the hall told me that the rebels had found the side staircase and had made their way to the second floor.

"If you find the king, kill him. Take what you can carry. Let them know we've been here!" someone yelled.

I moved as quietly as I could toward the resounding cheers, ducking into corners and surveying the hallway repeatedly. On one of the peeks back, I noticed two more uniforms. I motioned for them to get low and move slowly. As they got closer, I saw it was Avery and Tanner. I couldn't have asked for better backup. Avery was a hell of a shot, and Tanner always went above and beyond because he had more than most of us to lose if he didn't.

Tanner was one of the few officers who came into the service married. He had told us again and again how his wife complained that he wore his wedding ring on his thumb, but it was his grandfather's, and they had no means to resize it. He promised her it was the first thing he'd spend his money on when he got home, along with a better ring for her while he was at it.

She was his America. He was always focused because of her.

"What's going on?" Avery whispered.

"I think I just heard their leader. Ordered men to kill the king and steal what they could."

Tanner stood, holding his gun by his ear. "We need to find them, make sure they're heading up and away from the safe room."

I nodded. "There might be more than we can handle, but if we stay low, I think—"

At the other end of the hall, a door crashed open, and a butler raced out with two rebels behind him. It was the young butler, the one from the kitchen. He looked lost and horrified. The rebels were holding what looked like farm tools, so at least they wouldn't be able to fire back at us.

I turned, steadied my weight, and aimed. "Down!" I shouted, and the butler obeyed. I shot, hitting one of the rebels in his leg. Avery got the other, but his shot, intentional or not, looked much more deadly.

"I'm going to secure them," Avery said. "Find the leader."

I watched the butler stand and bolt for a bedroom, not caring that anyone could easily get in or out. He needed the illusion of safety.

I heard more shouts, more guns going off, and knew this was going to be one of the bad attacks. My mind became sharp, more focused. I had one mission, and that was all I could see.

Tanner and I crept up to the third floor, finding several side tables, art pieces, and plants already demolished. A rebel, using something like lumpy paint he must have brought with him, was writing something into the wall. I quickly moved up behind him and butted him in the head with the handle of my gun. He dropped, and I bent to check him for weapons.

A second later, a fresh wave of gunshots came at the other end of the hall, and Tanner dragged me behind a turned-up couch. When the noise died, we peeked out to assess the damage.

"I count six," he said.

"Same. I can get two, maybe three."

"That's enough. Remainders might rush. Or have guns."

I looked around. Taking a shard of broken mirror, I cut part of the couch's upholstery off and wrapped it around the glass. "Use this if they get too close."

"Nice," Tanner commented, then aimed his gun. I did the same.

The shots were quick, and we each took out two rebels before the two others turned, running toward us, not away. Remembering orders to keep rebels alive for questioning, I aimed at their legs, but with them moving so frantically, my shots all missed.

Tanner and I watched as a hulking man lumbered down Tanner's side of the hall, while an older guy, wiry and wild-eyed, came toward me. I holstered my gun, preparing myself for a fight.

"Damn. You got the good one," Tanner commented before launching himself over the chair and running full speed at his opponent.

I was a split second behind him. The older rebel came at me, yelling with his hands stretched out like claws. I grabbed one of his arms while using my makeshift knife to cut at his chest.

He wasn't the strongest thing, and part of me actually pitied him. When I latched on to his arm, I could feel his bones far too easily.

He whimpered and fell to his knees, and I pulled his arms behind him, securing both those and his legs with restraining bands. As I was tying them together, someone grabbed me from behind and slammed me into a nearby portrait, cutting my forehead on the glass.

I was dizzy and the blood was already leaking into my eyes, making it harder for me to face my enemy. I felt a thrill of panic before my training came back to me. I crouched as he held on to me from behind, and used my leverage to flip him over my shoulder.

Though he was much bigger than me, he crashed onto the debris-covered floor. I reached for more restraining bands only to collapse as another rebel barged into me.

I was pinned to the floor, my arms held down by a large man straddling my stomach.

His breath was swampy and foul as he spoke into my face.

"Take me to the king," he ordered, his voice like gravel.

I shook my head.

He released my arms, grabbing fistfuls of my jacket, and I reached up to push at his face. But he pulled me up by my clothes and slammed my head into the floor, making me drop my hands to the ground instantly. My head swam and my breathing felt off. The rebel palmed my skull, forcing me to face him.

"Where. Is. The. King?"

"Don't know," I gasped, fighting the ache in my head.

"Come on, pretty boy," he teased. "Give me the king, and I might let you live."

I couldn't mention the safe room. Even if I hated the things the king did, giving him away meant giving America away, and that was not an option.

I could lie. Maybe buy myself enough time to get out of this.

Or I could die.

"Fourth floor," I lied. "Hidden room in the east wing. Maxon's there, too."

He smiled, his disgusting breath coming out with his short laugh. "Now, that wasn't so hard, was it?"

I stayed silent.

"Maybe if you'd told me the first time I asked, I wouldn't have to do this."

He laced his hands gruffly around my throat, squeezing. On top of my already cloudy head, this was torture. My legs flailed, and I bucked my hips, trying to throw him off. It was pointless. He was simply too big.

I felt my limbs stop working, all oxygen escaping my system.

Who would tell my mother?

Who would take care of my family?

. . . at least I kissed America one last time.

. . . one last time.

. . . time.

Through the haze, I heard the gun go off and felt the massive rebel go limp and fall to the side. My throat made bizarre noises as it pulled air into my body again.

"Leger? You okay?"

My eyes were going black, so I couldn't make out Avery's face. But I heard him. And that was enough.

CHAPTER 11

THE DEBRIEFING WAS HELD IN the hospital wing, since so many officers had ended up there.

"We feel it's a success that we lost only two men tonight," our commander said. "Considering their forces, it's a testament to your training and personal skill that more of you weren't killed."

He paused, like maybe we should applaud, but we were too worn down for that.

"We have twenty-three rebels contained for sentencing after being interrogated, which is fantastic. However, I'm disappointed at the body count." He stared us down. "Seventeen. Seventeen rebels dead."

Avery ducked his head. He'd already confessed that two of those were his.

"You are not to kill unless you or another officer is being

directly threatened, or if you see a rebel attacking a member of the royal family. We need this scum alive for questioning."

I heard a few quiet huffs throughout the wing. This was one order I didn't like. We could end things so much faster if we simply eliminated the rebels that came into the palace. But the king wanted his answers, and rumor had it there were particular ways he tortured information out of rebels. I hoped never to learn what those ways were.

"That said, you all did an excellent job protecting the palace and subduing the threat against it. Unless you are one of the few with serious injuries, your posts for the day are the same as originally scheduled. Get sleep if you can, and get ready. It's going to be a long day with the state the palace is in."

The head butler thought it would be best to have the royal family and the Elite do their work outside while the staff worked to get the palace back into a presentable shape. The women of the German Federation and the Italian monarchy were coming in a handful of days and the maids were already overwhelmed with preparations.

Between the glaring sun, exhaustion, and my starched uniform, I was already uncomfortable. Add the searing pain from the gash in my head, hidden bruises from being strangled, and some damage I couldn't even remember getting in my leg, and I was just plain miserable.

The only good thing about this day was that the setup allowed me to be near America. I watched as she sat with

Kriss, planning their upcoming event. Besides Celeste, I'd never seen America upset at one of the other girls, but everything about her body language today suggested that she was unhappy with Kriss. Kriss, however, looked completely oblivious as she chatted to America and peeked over at Maxon time and again. It bothered me a little that America followed Kriss's gaze, but I doubted her feelings were changing. How could she ever look at him and not see Marlee screaming?

The tents and tables around the lawn almost made it look like the royal family was hosting a garden party. Had I not seen it myself, I wouldn't have guessed that the palace had been ransacked. Everyone here tended to forget about the attacks and move on.

I couldn't figure out if that was because dwelling on the attacks only made them that much more terrifying or if there was simply no time. It occurred to me that if the royal family really stopped and thought about the attacks, maybe they'd find a better way of preventing them.

"Don't know why I even bother," the king said a little too loudly. He handed a paper to someone and gave them a quiet order. "Erase Maxon's marks on this; they're distracting."

While the words filled my ears, America's gaze took all of my sight. She watched me carefully. I could tell she was worried about the bandages on my head, the limp in my steps. I gave her a wink, hoping to calm her nerves. I wasn't sure if I could make it through a whole day on rounds and then switch with someone to guard her door tonight, but if that was my only way to—

"Rebels! Run!"

I turned my head toward the palace doors, sure someone was confused.

"What?" Markson called.

"Rebels! Inside the palace!" Lodge yelled. "They're coming!"

I watched the queen bolt upright and run around the side of the palace, heading for a secret entrance under the protection of her maids.

The king snatched up his papers. If I was him, I'd be more worried about my neck than any lost information, no matter what those documents said.

America was still in her chair, paralyzed. I took a step to go get her, but Maxon jumped in front of me, shoving Kriss into my arms.

"Run!" he ordered. I hesitated, thinking of America. "Run!"

I did what I had to and bolted as Kriss called out to Maxon over and over again. A split second later, I heard gunshots and saw a swarm of people flood out of the palace, almost an equal mix of soldiers and rebels.

"Tanner!" I yelled, stopping him as he headed toward the fray. I shoved Kriss in his arms. "Follow the queen."

He obeyed without question, and I turned to get Mer.

"America! No! Come back!" Maxon screamed. I followed his panicked gaze and saw America running frantically toward the forest, rebels fast on her heels.

No.

The staccato rhythm of the guards firing accentuated America's pace, hurried and perilous. The rebels were nearly on top of her, bags stuffed. They seemed younger and fitter than the group last night, and I wondered if these were their children, trying to finish what their parents started.

I pulled out my gun and took my stance. I had my eye trained on the back of a rebel's head, and I fired three quick shots. They all missed when the guy zigzagged and ran behind a tree.

Maxon took a few desperate steps in the direction of the forest, but his father grabbed him before he got very far.

"Stand down!" Maxon yelled, pushing out of his father's grasp. "You'll hit her. Cease fire!"

Though America wasn't a member of the royal family, I doubted anyone would be upset if we killed these rebels without questioning. I ran into the field, took my stance again, and shot twice. Nothing.

Maxon's hands gripped my collar. "I said stand down!"

While I was an inch or two taller than he was, and I generally thought him to be a coward, the rage in his eyes at that moment demanded respect.

"Forgive me, sir."

He released me with a push, turning around and running his hand through his hair. I'd never seen him pace like that. It reminded me of his father when he was on the verge of exploding.

Everything he was showing on the outside, I felt on the

inside. One of his Elite was gone; the only girl I'd ever loved was missing. I didn't know if she would be able to outrun the rebels or find a place to hide. My heart was racing with fear and falling apart in hopelessness at the same time.

I'd promised May I wouldn't let anyone hurt her. I'd failed.

I looked behind me, not sure what I was expecting to see. The girls and staff had all made it to safety. No one remained but the prince, the king, and a dozen or so guards.

Maxon finally looked up at us, and his expression reminded me of a caged animal. "Get her. Get her now!" he screamed.

I debated just running into the forest, wanting to reach America before anyone else did. But how would I find her?

Markson stepped forward. "Come on, boys. Let's get organized." We followed him into the field.

My steps were sluggish and I tried to steady myself. I needed to be sharp today. *We're going to find her,* I promised myself. *She's tougher than anyone knows.*

"Maxon, go to your mother," I heard the king order.

"You can't be serious. How am I supposed to sit in some safe room while America's missing? She could be dead." I turned back to see Maxon double over and heave, nearly throwing up over the thought.

King Clarkson pulled him upright, gripping him firmly at the shoulders and shaking him. "Get it together. We need you safe. Go. Now."

Maxon balled his fists, slightly bending his elbows, and for a split second, I genuinely thought he was about to punch his father.

Maybe it wasn't my place, but I felt certain the king could demolish Maxon if he had the inclination. I didn't want the guy to die.

After a few charged breaths, Maxon wrenched himself out of his father's grasp and stomped into the palace.

I whipped my head around, hoping the king wouldn't realize someone had noticed that interaction. I was wondering more and more about the king's dissatisfaction with his son, but after that, I couldn't help but think things went much deeper than Maxon scribbling the wrong notes on his paperwork.

Why would someone so concerned with his son's safety be so . . . aggressive toward him?

I caught up to the other officers just as Markson started talking. "Are any of you familiar with this forest?"

We all stood silent.

"It's very large, and branches into a wide spread of trees just a few feet in, as you can see. The palace walls go back about four hundred feet before curving in to meet, but the wall toward the back of the forest has been in disrepair. It wouldn't be too hard for the rebels to get over a damaged portion, especially considering how easily they got over the strongest sections at the front."

Well, perfect.

"We're going to spread out in a line and walk slowly. Look for footprints, dropped goods, bent branches, anything that could be a clue to where they've taken her. If it gets too dark, we'll come back for flashlights and fresh men."

He eyed us all. "I do not want to come back empty-handed. Either with the lady alive or with her body, we are not leaving the king or prince without answers tonight, do you understand me?"

"Yes, sir," I yelled, and the others joined.

"Good. Spread out."

We had only moved a few yards when Markson held out a hand, stopping me.

"That's a pretty serious limp, Leger. Are you up for this?" he asked.

My blood drained, and I pictured myself going into a rage much like Maxon had. There was no way in hell I wasn't going.

"I'm perfectly fine, sir," I vowed.

Markson looked me over again. "We need a strong team for this. Maybe you should stay behind."

"No, sir," I answered quickly. "I've never disobeyed an order, sir. Don't make me do it now."

My eyes were dead serious, and I was sure that was what he saw when I stared him down, determined to go. There was a half smile on his face when he nodded and started heading toward the trees.

"Fine. Let's go."

Everything felt like it was moving in slow motion. We would call out for America, and stop to listen for a reply, finding ourselves fooled by the slightest motion or breeze. Someone would find a footprint, but the dirt was so dry, the mark would have disintegrated into nothing two steps later, leaving us with little more than wasted time. Twice we found scraps of clothes caught in low branches, but nothing matched what America was wearing. The worst was the few drops of blood we found. We stopped for an hour to look through every cloistered tree, explore any speck of dirt that might have been upturned.

The evening was coming on, and soon we would lose the light.

While the others marched forward, I stood still for a minute. In any other scenario, I would have found this beautiful. The light filtered down, almost like it wasn't sunshine at all, but its ghost. The trees reached for one another, like they were desperate for company, and the entire feeling of the place was somewhat haunting.

And I had to brace myself for the possible reality that I would leave this place and not have her with me. Worse, I might leave it carrying her body.

The thought was crippling. What would I fight for in this world if I wasn't fighting for her?

I was trying to look for the good. She was the only good in me.

I bit back the tears and stood strong. I would just have to keep fighting.

"Be sure to look everywhere," Markson reminded us. "If they've killed her, they might have hung her or tried to bury her. Pay attention."

His words made me feel sick again, but I pushed past them. "Lady America!" I cried out.

"I'm here!" I trained my ears on the sound, too afraid to believe. "I'm over here!"

America came running, shoeless and dirty, and I holstered my gun to open my arms for her.

"Thank goodness." I sighed. I wanted to kiss her then and there. But she was breathing and in my arms, and that would have to be enough. "I've got her! She's alive!" I called to the others, watching as the uniforms came toward us.

She was trembling a little, and I could tell she was stunned from the whole experience.

Injured leg or not, I was keeping her in my arms no matter what. I cradled her to me, and she put her hands behind my head, holding on. "I was terrified we were going to find your body somewhere," I confessed. "Are you hurt?"

"My legs a little."

I peeked down, and there were some bloody cuts. All things considered, we were lucky.

Markson stopped in front of us, trying to contain his happiness at finding her. "Lady America, are you injured at all?"

"Just some scratches on my legs."

"Did they try to hurt you?" he continued.

"No. They never caught up to me."

That's my girl.

All the faces wore gleefully shocked expressions at this news, but Markson was by far the happiest. "None of the other girls could have outrun them, I don't think."

America let out a breath and smiled. "None of the other girls is a Five."

I laughed, hearing the others do the same. Not every experience in the lowers was useless.

"Good point." Markson gave me a pat on the shoulder while he looked at America. "Let's get you back." He led the way, shouting out more instructions.

"I know you're fast and smart, but I was terrified," I told her as we moved.

She put her mouth to my ear. "I lied to the officer."

"What do you mean?" I whispered back.

"They did catch up with me, eventually." I stared at her, wondering what was so bad that she didn't want to confess it in front of the others. "They didn't do anything, but this one girl saw me. She curtsied and ran off."

Relief set in. Then confusion. "Curtsied?"

"I was surprised, too. She didn't look angry or threatening at all. In fact, she just looked like a normal girl." She paused a minute before adding, "She had books, lots of them."

"That seems to happen a lot," I told her. "No clue what they're doing with them. My guess is kindling. I think it's cold where they stay."

It seemed more and more apparent that the rebels just wanted to ruin everything the palace had—its fine things, its walls, even its sense of safety—and taking the king's prized possessions for the sake of having something to burn seemed like a big middle finger to the monarchy.

Had I not seen how cruel they could be firsthand, I would have found it funny.

The others were so close that we kept silent for the rest of the trip, but the walk felt much shorter with America in my arms. I wished it was longer. After today, I didn't want her anywhere I couldn't see her.

"The next few days might be busy for me, but I'll try to come see you soon," I whispered as the palace came into view. I'd have to give her back to them now.

She tilted in toward me. "Okay."

"Take her to Doctor Ashlar, Leger, and you're off duty. Good job today," Markson said, slapping my back again.

The halls were still full of staff cleaning up from the first attack, and the nurses were so quick when we got to the hospital wing that I didn't get to speak to America again. But as I laid her on the bed, looking at her tattered dress and sliced legs, I couldn't help but think this was all my fault. When I traced the steps back to the very start, I knew that it was. I had to start making up for it.

America was sleeping when I crept into the hospital wing that night. She was cleaner, but her face still seemed worried, even at rest.

"Hey, Mer," I whispered, rounding her bed. She didn't stir. I didn't dare sit, not even with the excuse of checking on the girl I rescued. I stood in the freshly pressed uniform I would only wear for the few minutes it took to deliver this message.

I reached out to touch her, but then pulled back. I looked into her sleeping face and spoke.

"I—I came to tell you I'm sorry. About today, I mean." I sucked in a deep breath. "I should have run for you. I should have protected you. I didn't, and you could have died."

Her lips pursed and unpursed as she dreamed.

"Honestly, I'm sorry for a lot more than that," I admitted. "I'm sorry I got mad in the tree house. I'm sorry I ever said to send in the stupid form. It's just that I have this idea . . . " I swallowed. "I have this idea that maybe you were the only one I could make everything right for.

"I couldn't save my dad. I couldn't protect Jemmy. I can barely keep my family afloat, and I just thought that maybe I could give you a shot at a life that would be better than the one that I would have been able to give you. And I convinced myself that was the right way to love you."

I watched her, wishing I had the nerve to confess this while she could argue back with me and tell me how wrong I'd been.

"I don't know if I can undo it, Mer. I don't know if we'll ever be the same as we used to be. But I won't stop trying. You're it for me," I said with a shrug. "You're the only thing I've ever wanted to fight for."

There was so much more to say, but I heard the door to the hospital wing open. Even in the dark, Maxon's suit was impossible to miss. I started walking away, head down, trying to look like I was just on a round.

He didn't acknowledge me, barely even noticed me as he

moved to America's bed. I watched him pull up a chair and settle in beside her.

I couldn't help but be jealous. From that first day in her brother's apartment—from the very moment I knew how I felt about America—I'd been forced to love her from afar. But Maxon could sit beside her, touch her hand, and the gap between their castes didn't matter.

I paused by the door, watching. While the Selection had frayed the line between America and me, Maxon himself was a sharp edge, capable of cutting the string entirely if he got too close. But I couldn't get a clear idea of just how near America was letting him.

All I could do was wait and give America the time she seemed to need. Really, we all needed it.

Time was the only thing that would settle this.

Turn the page for a sneak peek
at the thrilling conclusion to
THE SELECTION SERIES

CHAPTER 1

THIS TIME WE WERE IN the Great Room enduring another etiquette lesson when bricks came flying through the window. Elise immediately hit the ground and started crawling for the side door, whimpering as she went. Celeste let out a high-pitched scream and bolted toward the back of the room, barely escaping a shower of glass. Kriss grabbed my arm, pulling me, and I broke into a run alongside her as we made our way to the exit.

"Hurry, ladies!" Silvia cried.

Within seconds, the guards had lined up at the windows and were firing, and the bursts of sound echoed in my ears as we fled. Whether they came with guns or stones, anyone showing the smallest level of aggression within sight of the palace would die. There was no more patience left for these attacks.

"I hate running in these shoes," Kriss muttered, a heap of dress draped over her arm, eyes focused on the end of the hall.

"One of us is going to have to get used to it," Celeste said, her breath labored.

I rolled my eyes. "If it's me, I'll wear sneakers every day. I'm already over this."

"Less talking, more moving!" Silvia yelled.

"How do we get downstairs from here?" Elise asked.

"What about Maxon?" Kriss huffed.

Silvia didn't answer. We followed her through a maze of hallways, looking for a path to the basement, watching as guard after guard ran in the opposite direction. I found myself admiring them, wondering at the courage it took to run *toward* danger for the sake of other people.

The guards passing us were completely indistinguishable from one another until a set of green eyes locked with mine. Aspen didn't look afraid or even startled. There was a problem, and he was on his way to fix it. That was simply who he was.

Our gaze was brief, but it was enough. It was like that with Aspen. In a split second, without a word, I could tell him *Be careful and stay safe.* And saying nothing, he'd answer *I know, just take care of yourself.*

While I could easily be at peace with the things we didn't need to say, I had no such luck with the things we'd said out loud. Our last conversation wasn't exactly a happy one. I had been about to leave the palace and had asked him to give me some space to get over the Selection. And then I'd ended up staying and had given him no explanation as to why.

Maybe his patience with me was falling short, his ability to see only the best in me running dry. Somehow I would have to fix that. I couldn't see a life for me that didn't include Aspen. Even now, as I hoped Maxon would choose me, a world without Aspen felt unimaginable.

"Here it is!" Silvia called, pushing a mysterious panel in a wall.

We started down the stairs, Elise and Silvia heading the charge.

"Damn it, Elise, pick up the pace!" Celeste yelled. I wanted to be irritated that she said it, but I knew we were all thinking the same thing.

As we descended into the darkness, I tried to reconcile myself to the hours that would be wasted, hiding like mice. We continued on, the sound of our escape covering the shouts until one man's voice rang out right on top of us.

"Stop!" he yelled.

Kriss and I turned together, watching as the uniform became clear. "Wait," she called to the girls below. "It's a guard."

We stood on the steps, breathing heavily. He finally reached us, gasping himself.

"Sorry, ladies. The rebels ran as soon as the shots were fired. Weren't in the mood for a fight today, I guess."

Silvia, running her hands over her clothes to smooth

them, spoke for us. "Has the king deemed it safe? If not, you're putting these girls in a very dangerous position."

"The head of the guard cleared it. I'm sure His Majesty—"

"You don't speak for the king. Come on, ladies, keep moving."

"Are you serious?" I asked. "We're going down there for nothing."

She fixed me with a stare that might have stopped a rebel in his tracks, and I shut my mouth. Silvia and I had built a friendship of sorts as she unknowingly helped me distract myself from Maxon and Aspen with her extra lessons. After my little stunt on the *Report* a few days ago, it seemed that had dissolved into nothing. Turning to the guard, she continued. "Get an official order from the king, and we'll return. Keep walking, ladies."

The guard and I shared an exasperated look and parted ways.

Silvia showed absolutely no remorse when, twenty minutes later, a different guard came, telling us we were free to go upstairs.

I was so irritated by the whole situation, I didn't wait for Silvia or the other girls. I climbed the stairs, exiting somewhere on the first floor, and continued to my room with my shoes still hooked on my fingers. My maids were missing, but a small silver platter holding an envelope was waiting on the bed.

I recognized May's handwriting instantly and tore open the envelope, devouring her words.

Ames,

We're aunts! Astra is perfect. I wish you were here to meet her in person, but we all understand you need to be at the palace right now. Do you think we'll be together for Christmas? Not that far away! I've got to get back to helping Kenna and James. I can't believe how pretty she is! Here's a picture for you. We love you!

May

I slipped the glossy photo from behind the note. Everyone was there except for Kota and me. James, Kenna's husband, was beaming, standing over his wife and daughter with puffy eyes. Kenna sat upright in the bed, holding a tiny pink bundle, looking equal parts thrilled and exhausted. Mom and Dad were glowing with pride, while May's and Gerad's enthusiasm jumped from the image. Of course Kota wouldn't have gone; there was nothing for him to gain from being present. But I should have been there.

I wasn't though.

I was here. And sometimes I didn't understand why. Maxon was still spending time with Kriss, even after all he'd done to get me to stay. The rebels unrelentingly attacked our safety from the outside, and inside, the king's icy words did just as much damage to my confidence. All the while, Aspen orbited me, a secret I had to keep. And the cameras came and went, stealing pieces of our lives to entertain the people. I was being pushed into a corner from every angle, and I was missing out on all the things that had always mattered to me.

I choked back angry tears. I was so tired of crying.

Instead I went into planning mode. The only way to set things right was to end the Selection.

Though I still occasionally questioned my desire to be the princess, there was no doubt in my mind that I wanted to be Maxon's. If that was going to happen, I couldn't sit back and wait for it. Remembering my last conversation with the king, I paced as I waited for my maids.

I could hardly breathe, so I knew eating would be a waste. But it would be worth the sacrifice. I needed to make some progress, and I needed to do it fast. According to the king, the other girls were making advances toward Maxon—physical advances—and he'd said I was far too plain to have a chance of matching them in that department.

As if my relationship with Maxon wasn't complicated enough, there was a whole new issue of rebuilding trust. And I wasn't sure if that meant I wasn't supposed to ask questions or not. While I felt pretty sure he hadn't gone that far physically with the other girls, I couldn't help but wonder. I'd never tried to be seductive before—pretty much every intimate moment I'd had with Maxon came about without intention—but I had to hope that if I was deliberate, I could make it clear that I was just as interested in him as the others.

I took a deep breath, raised my chin, and walked into the dining hall. I was purposely a minute or two late, hoping everyone would already be seated. I was right on that count. But the reaction was better than I'd hoped.

I curtsied, swinging my leg around so the slit in the dress fell open, leading nearly all the way up my thigh. The dress was a deep red, strapless and practically backless, and I was almost positive my maids had used magic to make it stay up at all. I rose, locking eyes with Maxon, who I noticed had stopped chewing. Someone dropped a fork.

Lowering my gaze, I walked to my seat, settling in next to Kriss.

"Seriously, America?" she whispered.

I tilted my head in her direction. "I'm sorry?" I replied, feigning confusion.

She put her silverware down, and we stared at each other. "You look trashy."

"Well, you look jealous."

I'd hit pretty close to the mark, because she flushed a bit before returning to her food. I took limited bites of my own, already miserably constricted. As dessert was being set in front of me, I chose to stop ignoring Maxon, and as I had hoped, his eyes were on me. He reached up and grabbed his ear immediately, and I demurely did the same. My gaze flickered quickly toward King Clarkson, and I tried not to smile. He was irritated, another trick I'd managed to get away with.

I excused myself first, giving Maxon a chance to admire the back of the dress, and scurried to my room. I closed the door to my room behind me and unzipped the gown immediately, desperate for a breath.

"How'd it go?" Mary asked, rushing over.

"He seemed stunned. They all did."

Lucy squealed, and Anne came to help Mary. "We'll hold it up. Just walk," she ordered. I did as I was told. "Is he coming tonight?"

"Yes. I'm not sure when, but he'll definitely be here." I perched on the edge of my bed, arms folded around my stomach to keep the open dress from falling down.

Anne gave me a sad face. "I'm sorry you'll have to be uncomfortable for a few more hours. I'm sure it'll be worth it though."

I smiled, trying to look like I was fine dealing with the pain. I'd told my maids I wanted to get Maxon's attention. I'd left out my hope that, with any luck, this dress would be on the floor pretty soon.

"Do you want us to stay until he arrives?" Lucy asked, her enthusiasm bubbling over.

"No, just help me zip this thing back up. I need to think some things through," I answered, standing so they could help me.

Mary took hold of the zipper. "Suck it in, miss." I obeyed, and as the dress cinched me in again, I thought of a soldier going to war. Different armor but the same idea.

Tonight I was taking down a man.

CHAPTER 2

I OPENED THE BALCONY DOORS, letting the air sweeten my room. Even though it was December, the breeze was light and tickled my skin. We weren't allowed to go outside at all anymore, not without guards by our sides, so this would have to do.

I scurried around the room, lighting candles, trying to make the space inviting. The knock came at the door, and I blew out the match, bolted over to the bed, picked up a book, and fanned out my dress. *Why yes, Maxon, this is how I always look when I read.*

"Come in," I offered, barely loud enough to be heard.

Maxon entered, and I lifted my head delicately, catching the wonder in his eyes as he surveyed my dimly lit room. Finally he focused on me, his gaze traveling up my exposed leg.

"There you are," I said, closing the book and standing to greet him.

He closed the door and came in, his eyes locked on my curves. "I wanted to tell you that you look fantastic tonight."

I flicked my hair over my shoulder. "Oh, this thing? It was just sitting in the back of the closet."

"I'm glad you pulled it out."

I laced my fingers through his. "Come sit with me. I haven't seen you much lately."

He sighed and followed. "I'm sorry about that. Things have been a bit tense since we lost so many people in that rebel attack, and you know how my father is. We sent several guards to protect your families, and our forces are stretched thin, so he's worse than usual. And he's pressuring me to end the Selection, but I'm holding my ground. I want to have some time to think this through."

We sat on the edge of the bed, and I settled close to him. "Of course. You should be in charge of this."

He nodded. "Exactly. I know I've said it a thousand times, but when people push me, it makes me crazy."

I gave him a little pout. "I know."

He paused, and I couldn't read his face. I was trying to figure out how to move this forward without being pushy, but I wasn't sure how to manufacture a romantic moment.

"I know this is silly, but my maids put this new perfume on me today. Is it too strong?" I asked, tilting my neck so he could lean in and breathe.

He came near, his nose hitting a soft patch of skin. "No,

dear, it's lovely," he said into the curve that led to my shoulder. Then he kissed me there. I swallowed, trying to focus. I needed to have some level of control.

"I'm glad you like it. I've really missed you."

I felt his hand snake around my back, and I brought my face down. There he was, eyes looking into mine, our lips millimeters apart.

"How much have you missed me?" he breathed.

His stare, combined with his voice being so low, was doing funny things to my heartbeat. "So much," I whispered back. "So, so much."

I leaned forward, aching to be kissed. Maxon was confident, pulling me closer with one hand and stringing the other through my hair. My body wanted to melt into the kiss, but the dress stopped me. Then, suddenly nervous again, I remembered my plan.

Sliding my hands down Maxon's arms, I guided his fingers to the zipper on the back of my dress, hoping that would be enough.

His hands lingered there for a moment, and I was seconds away from just asking him to unzip it when he burst out laughing.

The sound sobered me up pretty quickly.

"What's so funny?" I asked, horrified, trying to think of an inconspicuous way to check my breath.

"Of everything you've done, this is by far the most entertaining!" Maxon bent over, hitting his knee as he laughed.

"Excuse me?"

He kissed me hard on my forehead. "I always wondered what it would be like to see you try." He started laughing again. "I'm sorry; I have to go." Even the way he stood held a sense of amusement. "I'll see you in the morning."

And then he left. He just left!

I sat there, completely mortified. Why in the world did I think I could pull that off? Maxon may not know everything about me, but at the very least he knew my character—and this? It wasn't me.

I looked down at the ridiculous dress. It was way too much. Even Celeste wouldn't have gone this far. My hair was too perfect, my makeup too heavy. He knew what I was trying to do from the second he walked through the doorway. Sighing, I went around the room, blowing out candles and wondering how I was supposed to face him tomorrow.

CHAPTER 3

I DEBATED CLAIMING THE STOMACH flu. Or an incapacitating headache. Panic attack. Really, anything to get out of going to breakfast.

Then I thought of Maxon and how he always talked about putting on a brave face. That wasn't a particular strength of mine. But if I went downstairs at least, if I could just be present, maybe he'd give me some credit.

In hopes that I could erase some of what I'd done, I asked my maids to put me in the most demure dress I had. Based on that request alone, they knew not to ask about the night before. The neckline was a bit higher than the ones we typically wore in the warm Angeles weather, and it had sleeves that went nearly to my elbows. It was flowery and cheerful, the opposite of last night's getup.

I could barely look at Maxon when I entered the dining

hall, but I walked tall at least.

When I finally peeked at him, he was watching me, grinning. As he chewed his food, he winked at me; and I ducked my head again, pretending to be very interested in my quiche.

"Glad to see you in actual clothes today," Kriss spat.

"Glad to see you in such a good mood."

"What in the world has gotten into you?" she hissed.

Dejected, I gave up. "I'm not up for this today, Kriss. Just leave me alone."

For a moment, she looked as if she might fight back, but I guessed I wasn't worth it. She sat up a little straighter and continued eating. If I'd had any level of success last night, then I could justify my actions; as it was, I couldn't even fake being proud.

I risked another glance at Maxon, and even though he wasn't watching me, he was still suppressing a smug expression as he cut his food. That was it. I wasn't going to suffer through a day like this. I was about to swoon or clutch my stomach or do anything to get me out of the room when a butler came in. He carried an envelope on a silver platter, and he bowed before placing it in front of King Clarkson.

The king took the letter and read it quickly. "Damn French," he muttered. "Sorry, Amberly, it looks like I'll be leaving within the hour."

"Another problem with the trade agreement?" she asked quietly.

"Yes. I thought we'd settled all this months ago. We need

to be firm on this one." He stood, throwing his napkin on his plate, and made his way to the door.

"Father," Maxon called, standing. "Don't you want me to come?"

It had struck me as odd that the king didn't bark out a command for his son to follow when he exited, seeing as that was his usual method of instructing. Instead he turned to Maxon, his eyes cold and his voice sharp.

"When you're ready to behave the way a king should, you'll get to experience what a king does." Without saying anything more, he left us.

Maxon stood for a moment, shocked and embarrassed by his father's choice to call him out in front of everyone. As he sat down, he turned to his mother. "Wasn't really looking forward to that flight, if I'm being honest," he said, joking away the tension. The queen smiled, as of course she must, and the rest of us ignored it.

The other girls finished their breakfasts and excused themselves to the Women's Room. When it was just Maxon, Elise, and me remaining at our tables, I looked up at him. We both tugged our ears at the same time, then smiled. Elise finally left, and we met in the middle of the room, not bothered by the maids and butlers cleaning up around us.

"It's my fault he's not taking you," I lamented.

"Perhaps," he teased. "Trust me, this isn't the first time he's tried to put me in my place, and he has a million reasons in his head why he thinks he should. It wouldn't surprise me if his only motive this time was spite. He doesn't want to lose control, and the closer I am to picking a wife, the more of a likelihood that is for him. Though we both know he'll never truly let go."

"You might as well just send me home. He's never going to let you pick me." I still hadn't told Maxon about how his father had cornered me, threatening me in the middle of the hall after Maxon talked him into letting me stay. King Clarkson had made it clear I was to keep my mouth shut about our conversation, and I didn't want to cross him. At the same time, I hated keeping it from Maxon.

"Besides," I added, crossing my arms, "after last night, I can't imagine you're that keen on keeping me anyway."

He bit his lips. "I'm sorry I laughed, but really, what else could I do?"

"I had plenty of ideas," I muttered, still embarrassed at my attempt to seduce him. "I feel so stupid." I buried my head in my hands.

"Stop," he said gently, pulling me in for an embrace. "Trust me when I say, it was very tempting. But you're not that girl."

"But shouldn't I be? Shouldn't that be part of what we are?" I whined into his chest.

"Don't you remember the night in the safe room?" he said, his voice low.

"Yes, but that was basically us saying good-bye."

"It would have been a fantastic good-bye."

I stepped away and swatted at him. He laughed, happy to have broken through the uneasiness.

"Let's forget about it," I proposed.

"Very well," he agreed. "Besides, we have a project to work on, you and I."

"We do?"

"Yes, and since my father is gone, this will be a convenient time to start brainstorming."

"All right," I said, excited to be a part of something that was just between the two of us.

He sighed, making me nervous about what he was planning. "You're right. Father doesn't approve of you. But he might be forced to bend if we can manage one thing."

"Which is?"

"We have to make you the people's favorite."

I rolled my eyes. "*That* is what we're working on? Maxon, that's never going to happen. I saw a poll in one of Celeste's magazines after I tried to save Marlee. People can hardly stand me."

"Opinions change. Don't let that one moment bring you down too much."

I still felt hopeless, but what could I say? If this was my only option, I had to at least try.

"Fine," I said. "But I'm telling you, this won't work."

With an impish grin on his face, he came very close and gave me a long, slow kiss. "And I'm telling you it will."

THE SELECTION STORIES

❧·❧

BONUS CONTENT

- Q&A with Kiera Cass
- The Chosen Girls: A Complete List of the Selected
- What Makes a One: The List of Castes
- America Singer's Family Tree
- Aspen Leger's Family Tree
- Maxon Schreave's Family Tree
- *The Selection*: The Official Playlist
- *The Elite*: The Official Playlist

Q&A *with* KIERA CASS

❧

What was your favorite book growing up?

Oddly enough, I don't remember having any favorites. I do know my parents got me these Disney books that also came with a tape that said the words aloud, so I could follow along before I could actually read. I also remember that I was able to read earlier than most of my friends, and I would read to the other kids at my day care.

That's so funny. I'd forgotten about all of that until now. But I guess I liked books from the very start!

When did you realize you wanted to become a writer?

I kind of stumbled into it. I was going through some issues that I didn't quite know how to handle, and one day I just decided I was going to give them to a character and see what she did. Reading is a big coping mechanism of mine, so a story seemed like the right way to go, and it ended up giving me a lot of clarity. I never finished that project because lots of characters started popping into my head with their own stories to tell. America was, I think, third in line, but one of the first who demanded I write her story down.

What inspired The Selection?

The Selection was born out of wondering about the *what ifs* of other stories, mainly Esther (from the Bible) and Cinderella. I wondered if Esther—before she was shipped off to the palace to compete for this king—maybe liked the boy next door. She wins, which is awesome, but even if she lost, she was never going home. Did she maybe care about someone else and have to let that love die? I've always been curious about her heart. And Cinderella never asked for a prince. She asked for a night off and a dress. We assume that she lived happily ever after because she got a man, but what if that wasn't the case? What if being a princess was way more than she was prepared to deal with?

Those two thoughts married in my head, and I knew I wanted to write a story about a girl who would come from a humble background and would gain the attention of a prince, but she wouldn't want him because she was already in love. And I knew that she would go through something that would show her more of the world than she was ever prepared to see, and that thing ended up being the Selection.

What's been the best fan reaction to the series that you've received so far?

As far as real life goes, I had a reader come to a signing with her copies of *The Selection* and *The Elite* with about fifty sticky notes hanging out of each of them. Then she and maybe eight other people hung around afterward asking serious questions about the characters and the world. I had no idea people would be paying so much attention. Also at that same signing a girl came with Coke Zero and Wheat Thins (my writing snacks of choice) attempting to bribe me to make sure America ended up with Aspen. So cute!

Online, Tumblr has shocked me! People have made incredible art, created role-playing sites, written fan fics, and come up with wonderful theories for the final book. It's really cool because I do this alone in my office, so to see other people as excited as I am NEVER gets old. So much fun!

How do you choose names for your characters?

Almost all of them are rejected baby names. Amberly, Kamber, Tuesday, Emmica, and even America were all baby girl names that my hubby said no to. So I gave them to my fictional babies, where they'd be safe.

Every once in a while, I go hunting for a name. Aspen came about as I searched for a rugged but kind of romantic-sounding name. Fact: I almost changed his name to Apsen because I kept spelling it wrong. And sometimes I borrow names from friends or from awesome readers. There are at least five names that have come from early fans across the three books.

What was the toughest part of the series to write?

As far as working goes, the entire second book was difficult. People had told me sequels were hard, but I was having none of it. I liked what was happening . . . but ended up taking the entire middle of the book out. Twice. There are still days when I look for plot points in the story that never happened on paper.

As far as emotional writing, the last several chapters of *The One* were very hard to write on many levels for me.

What was the very first scene of The Selection that you wrote?

The very first line in the book. It was clear that this girl had just gotten a letter that was about to change her life, and she wanted nothing to do with it. The entire first book was written chronologically with me asking America, "So what happened next?" every time I got to the end of what felt like a chapter. *The Elite* was written in scenes and then all strung together, and with *The One*, I started at the end and worked my way backward.

Describe America in six words.

Beginning of Book One: Please don't make me do this.
End of Book Two: Wait . . . can I really do this?

Describe Aspen in six words.

Beginning of Book One: I'll never give up on you.
End of Book Two: Please don't give up on me.

Describe Maxon in six words.

Beginning of Book One: God, I hope they like me.
End of Book Two: Wait, now who do I like?

Which character in the series do you identify the most with?

May. I didn't realize it until much later, but she and I would be absolute BFFs in real life. She's almost fifteen, and all I want to do is look at magazines and listen to pop music with her. Not sure what that says about me as I'm in my thirties, but I don't even care. May is my girl.

Which character has surprised you the most in the series?

There were secrets about a lot of characters that I knew the whole time, so I wrote the first book through the eyes of the last. Not very much surprised me. But I will say, I didn't expect Kriss to get so vocal. In my eyes, she was there to hang out in the background, but once everything between Maxon and America started going downhill, she elbowed her way to the front of my head and demanded her chance.

Which event has surprised you the most in the series?

I knew Marlee had a secret early on, but it took me a while to figure out what it was and that it would be exposed. Once that became clear, I had to deal with the fact that she and Carter would be punished. I had to research canings, the types of rods used, the different styles of whippings, and the kind of injuries and scars it would leave behind.

Once I realized that was going to happen to Marlee, I had a hard time dealing with it. I would have to pause when I was writing, or I'd cry a little. I'm not sure if the event itself surprised me so much as me becoming aware of how attached I was to these little people inside my head. I really do suffer with them.

Are any of the characters based on people you know?

Yes and no. I definitely take traits from people, or at least feelings I have associated with their names. I knew a very unkind Celeste as a child, so when this mean girl walked into the airport, I knew her name in an instant. And I've borrowed tons of names from people I know, like my younger brother, Gerad. (For the record, though, he is very musical, and would be a pretty good Five.)

Probably the biggest pull is from Callaway, my husband. He's asked several times if Maxon was based off him, and the truth is kind of . . . but not really. There's a little bit of Callaway in every boy I write. How can there not be? He's my example of love; he's the guy I fell for. The things I find attractive in him tend to make their way to the page. Aspen's passion and devotion? Callaway. Maxon's nerdiness and sweetness? Callaway. Even the way Carter looks at people is shaded by the way Callaway does. I can't help it!

Have you always known how America's story would end?

Kind of. I self-published a book called *The Siren* in 2009, which followed a girl named Kahlen as she lived a temporary life of being a servant for the Ocean. Kahlen was a little bitter about her circumstances and wanted everyone to know her story. If I asked her a question, she answered without fail.

When America piped up and told me I should tell her

story next, I thought she would be the exact same way: eager to tell me everything. But she's a different person, and more often than not, I was putting words in her mouth. By the time I got to the end of the first book, I realized two things: One, I'd gotten her totally wrong and was going to have to go back and rewrite the book. And two, the person I thought she would end up with was not the person she actually chose.

I'd colored that decision based on my perception of her instead of taking the time to find out what she wanted. When I finally started to really hear her, it was obvious I was wrong. I can't wait for the final book to come out so I can share everything that unfolded in the original ending. It was super dramatic! I mean, totally wrong, but crazy dramatic.

If you lived in Illéa, would you want to enter the Selection?

It depends. Do I have an Aspen in my life? Is the prince up for grabs like Maxon? I think if I was a single girl, I'd maybe put my name in the running, but only if the prince in question seemed like a nice guy. I get that he's looking for love, but so am I! However, if there was already a guy in my life . . . I don't think I could.

Either way, I'd be an awful princess.

Where was America and Aspen's first kiss?

In the tree house.

Aspen, being a few years older, had already kissed a few girls around town. All the Six girls really hoped to get ahold of him, because, besides being absolutely handsome, Aspen had that "I could be bad but I choose not to be" air about him that always seemed to draw them in. None of those kisses really mattered, though, and when the spark kindled in his heart for America, he was determined to sweep her off her feet.

America, just about to turn fifteen, had never felt anything for anyone before, and she wasn't really sure what to make of this boy she'd known her whole life but had avoided, suddenly filling up every spare inch in her head and heart.

After Aspen gave America the card at her birthday party, they met in the tree house about every other day for two weeks, talking, joking, and sharing those tiny little touches that feel like the world when you're just learning some-one likes you. By the end of the second week, Aspen really couldn't take it anymore.

America was snuggled up next to him, with her head on his shoulder. On an impulse, Aspen cupped her cheek, turned her to him, and kissed her. Her eyes went wide, a little shocked to be receiving her first kiss, but Aspen held her there. It only took a few seconds for her to throw her arms around him and crawl in his lap. They did little else that night but kiss.

What is one thing about America that we wouldn't know from reading the books?

There are probably a bunch of tiny things that readers don't know, but I don't realize they don't know, because I

203

do, if that makes any sense. When a new detail pops up about Maxon or Aspen, it's as much a shock to me as it is to anyone because I see the story through America's eyes, not theirs. But it wouldn't surprise me at all to be talking about America being half-Jewish and people being like, "Really?" But I've been looking at her family tree for years now, so it's just obvious to me.

I feel like that's a lame answer, but it's true!

THE CHOSEN GIRLS:
A COMPLETE LIST OF THE SELECTED

❧•❧

- Marlee Tames from Kent, Four
- Elayna Stoles from Hansport, Three
- Tuesday Keeper from Waverly, Four
- Olivia Witts from Zuni, Three
- Fiona Castley from Paloma,Three
- Celeste Newsome from Clermont, Two
- Emmica Brass from Tammins, Four
- Samantha Lowell from Sonage, Three
- Tiny Lee from Dakota, Three
- Kriss Ambers from Columbia, Three
- Bariel Pratt from Sota, Two
- Ashley Brouillette from Allens, Three
- Janell Stanton from Likely, Three
- Amy Everheart from Atlin, Three
- Tallulah Bell from Hundson, Two
- Anna Farmer from Honduragua, Four
- Kayleigh Poulin from Sumner, Three
- Emily Arnold from Labrador, Three
- Elizabeth O'Brien from Fennley, Three
- Natalie Luca from Bankston, Four
- Lyssa Bow from Whites, Five
- Hannah Carver from Bonita, Five
- Elise Whisks from Angeles, Four
- Jenna Banks from Midston, Three
- Clarissa Kelley from Belcourt, Two
- C.C. Lands from St. George, Four
- Laila Toil from Panama, Four
- Reeli Tanner from Denbeigh, Four
- Mikaela Coveny from Calgary, Three
- Camille Astor from Baffin, Two
- Mia Blue from Ottaro, Three
- Zoe Peddler from Lakedon, Four
- Sosie Keeper from Yukon, Four
- Leah Sacks from Dominca, Three
- America Singer from Carolina, Five

WHAT MAKES A ONE:
THE LIST OF CASTES

❖

A note from Kiera: This is a general idea of where professions fall within the castes described in *The Selection.* I realize it doesn't cover every possible job on the planet, but hopefully this list makes the divisions a bit clearer.

ONES: Royalty, clergy

TWOS: All celebrities, such as MTV-type musicians, professional athletes, actors, models; politicians as well as all officers in any policing, military, firefighting, or guarding position that are assigned by draft

THREES: Educators of any kind, philosophers, inventors, writers, scientists of any kind, doctors, veterinarians, dentists, architects, librarians, all engineers, therapists or psychologists, film directors, music producers, lawyers

FOURS: Farm owners, jewelers, real-estate agents, insurance brokers, head chefs, project managers for construction, property/business owners for things like restaurants, shops, and hotels

FIVES: Classically trained musicians and singers, all artists, live theater actors, dancers, circus performers of any kind

SIXES: Secretaries, waitstaff, housekeepers, seamstresses, store clerks, cooks, drivers

SEVENS: Gardeners, construction workers, farmhands, gutter or pool cleaners, almost all outdoor workers

EIGHTS: The mentally or physically unwell (particularly if there is no one to care for them), addicts, runaways, the homeless

AMERICA SINGER'S FAMILY TREE

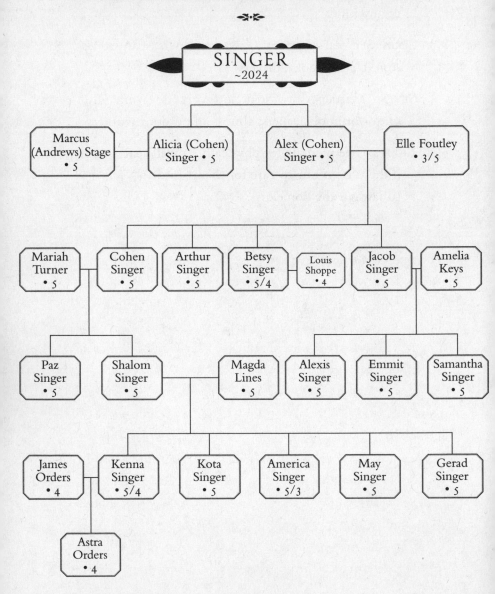

A note from Kiera: Alicia and Alex Cohen were twenty-two and twenty-four respectively when their father died in World War Four. Alex had just finished studying at Julliard while his sister was getting ready to enter medical school. When he got the notice that his name was being changed to Singer, and that he was now a Five, he didn't understand it, and disregarded the letter. The caste system was only something those in the upper tiers really knew about until after it happened.

His new fiancée, Elle, thought nothing of it, not caring that she was supposedly a Three now, but when the system rigidly locked down and her teaching license was revoked, she was heartbroken. Alicia was immediately kicked out of school and told she was an artist.

The Singer family tree is the most typical of those in Illéa. They've almost entirely married within the same caste and died relatively young. Even though their status is low, the Singer family is attractive and talented, so they do as best as a family of Fives could expect.

America's parents met while working. When Shalom sold six pieces to a wealthy Two, the man held a party to show off his new purchases, and Shalom was there to explain his art. Magda was hired to play piano in the background, and he was instantly drawn to her talent. She ignored his advances, hoping to marry up a caste or two, but eventually succumbed to his charm and attention.

Once Shalom and Magda started having children, the stress of the finances drove a wedge between them. While there has always been love in their marriage, there has also been a constant worry over money. Magda's greatest triumph to date is America gaining the status of a Three, and while America is away at the palace, Magda rubs it in the face of any of the families that have ever been unkind to them. It's only in the quietest times of their life that Magda can truly show Shalom that she still loves him.

America looks at love much the way her father does. She looks at a lot of things the way her father does and has always favored him.

Had the caste system not fallen into place, America's last name would be Cohen.

ASPEN LEGER'S FAMILY TREE

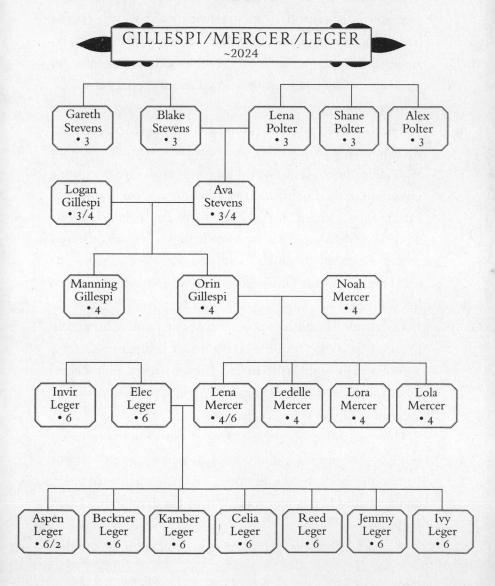

GILLESPI/MERCER/LEGER
~2024

Gareth Stevens • 3

Blake Stevens • 3

Lena Polter • 3

Shane Polter • 3

Alex Polter • 3

Logan Gillespi • 3/4

Ava Stevens • 3/4

Manning Gillespi • 4

Orin Gillespi • 4

Noah Mercer • 4

Invir Leger • 6

Elec Leger • 6

Lena Mercer • 4/6

Ledelle Mercer • 4

Lora Mercer • 4

Lola Mercer • 4

Aspen Leger • 6/2

Beckner Leger • 6

Kamber Leger • 6

Celia Leger • 6

Reed Leger • 6

Jemmy Leger • 6

Ivy Leger • 6

A note from Kiera: Aspen's family was almost untouched by the original caste implementation. Ava and Logan Gillespi lived a quiet life as Threes. They were both writers, and were devoutly patriotic. One of their neighbors was caught harboring rebels, and Gregory Illéa sentenced that family to Eights and made everyone on their block drop a caste, as he assumed someone must have known about the illegal activities and didn't tell.

The Gillespies, new to being Fours, made friends with the Mercers, a family who owned a restaurant. Seeing that as a viable option, they pooled their resources into opening a restaurant of their own, and their daughter, Orin, eventually married the Mercers' son, Noah. Orin and Noah had four daughters while, unbeknownst to them, Orin's parents saved so that the oldest daughter, Lena, could buy her way back to the Three status the family should have, and help the rest of her siblings.

Lena took the money . . . but spent most of it to pay for the fine so she could marry a server in their restaurant, a young man with brilliant green eyes named Elec Leger. They quietly endured the waiting period, married in secret, and returned to tell Lena's parents.

Lena was unceremoniously kicked out of her family, left with no one but Elec. They were homeless for five months before they both could save enough to get a small apartment, and that tiny home was soon full of children—very loved children.

Aspen watched his father die from a sickness he couldn't

even name because they were too broke to visit a doctor for a diagnosis. Within a month of falling ill, Elec was dead.

Lena mourned the loss of her husband deeply. But even though she was now parenting seven children alone with very little income, she never regretted her choice to marry Elec. There are no pictures of Aspen's father, but his things are around the house, and Aspen will often find his mother cleaning of a knickknack of his and lovingly setting it back in its place.

But Aspen also watches as she works herself to the bone. And that is the main reason he second-guesses his life with America. He loves her with a singular devotion, but in his eyes there's a huge difference between being born into his lifestyle and descending into it.

Prior to the caste system, the Leger family name was Huntington.

MAXON SCHREAVE'S FAMILY TREE

ILLÉA/SCHREAVE
~2024

Gregory Illéa • 1	Bethany Schreave • 1	Brenton Schreave • 1	Elizabeth Feller • 1

Brenton Schreave II • 1	Nicole Islay • 2/1	Henry Schreave • 1

Emil de Monpezat • 1	Katherine Illéa • 1	Spencer Illéa • 1	Damon Illéa • 1	Grace Lowell • 2/1

Antonella de Illéa de Monpezat • 1	Abby Tamblin • 3/1	Justin Illéa • 1	Porter Schreave • 1	Abby Illéa • 3/1

Aaron Station • 4/1	Ainsley Station • 4/1	Adele Station • 4/1	Amberley Station • 4/1	Clarkson Schreave • 1

Maxon Schreave • 1

A note from Kiera: The Schreaves have the typical drama of a royal family. Gregory always considered himself a cut above his closest friend, Brenton Schreave, but needed someone to bounce ideas off, and Brenton was his most suitable option. Gregory married Brenton's sister Bethany and began having children years before his transition into power. By the time he was in charge, he had tired of the responsibilities of being a husband and father. It's rumored the fall that took Bethany's life was more a suicide attempt than an accident.

Gregory arranged the marriage of his oldest child, Katherine, to the prince of Swendway, securing his role as king before turning to his sons. When Spencer mysteriously died a few years after his sister's marriage, all eyes fell to Damon, the youngest Illéa. With the nation's morale at a low after two royal deaths, a poor economy, and a mass of the citizens upset over the newly implemented caste system, the Selection was created to begin the new royal line and appease the public.

The first Selection was a complete setup. Damon slept with half the girls before sending them home the next day, eventually settling with Grace, who was his father's pick. Abby, the winner of the second Selection, liked Prince Justin just fine, but was more attracted to his cousin, Porter. They conspired together to kill Justin, and Gregory, who was close to death, encouraged her to marry Porter to continue the royal lineage.

Abby humbly accepted Porter's proposal, and she was pregnant with his son well before the wedding. But their passion for each other soon faded. If Abby could so easily dispose of her first husband, why not her second? Porter kept his distance, and their only son, Clarkson, grew up in a home full of screaming, accusations, and occasional violence.

Amberly was the star of her Selection, not because of her beauty or power, but because of her calming nature. The opposite of everything Clarkson had ever known, he was drawn to her from the start. When a small uprising happened in the south, Clarkson suggested to his father that marrying a girl from a lower caste might appease them, and their marriage did soothe some of the public.

Clarkson, however, has never overcome his trust issues. Amberly sees more than anyone else, but still doesn't know everything. Clarkson keeps his family under his control because he thinks it's normal. Amberly genuinely loves her husband and overlooks his flaws, and it's her disposition that keeps Maxon from completely following his father's example.

THE SELECTION:
THE OFFICIAL PLAYLIST

◆·◆

"FAIRYTALE" BY SARA BAREILLES
"I don't care for your fairytales."

"I didn't want to be royalty. And I didn't want to be a One.
I didn't even want to try."—Chapter 1

"DIRTY LITTLE SECRET" BY THE ALL-AMERICAN REJECTS
*"I'll keep you, my dirty little secret. Don't tell anyone or you'll
be just another regret."*

"So us being this personal and out well past Illéa's cur-
few . . . we could both get in serious trouble. Not to
mention the hell I'd get from my mother."—Chapter 2

"WHAT YOU WISH FOR" BY GUSTER
*"And what you wish for won't come true. You aren't surprised,
love, are you?"*

"'You know I can only agree to sign up, right? I can't make
them pick me?'
'Yes, I know. But it's worth a shot.'"—Chapter 3

"GOOD-BYE TO YOU" BY MICHELLE BRANCH
"You were the one I loved, the one thing that I tried to hold on to."

"He pulled me in tight and kissed me—really kissed

me—one last time. Then he disappeared into the night. And because this country is the way it is, because of all the rules that had kept us in hiding, I couldn't even call out after him. I couldn't tell him I loved him one more time."—Chapter 5

"Big Casino" by Jimmy Eat World
"I'll accept with poise, with grace, when they draw my name from the lottery."
"'Miss America Singer of Carolina, Five.'"—Chapter 5

"All I Wanted" by Paramore
"I could follow you to the beginning, just to relive the start."
"'I hate him! I loved you! I wanted you; all I ever wanted was you!'"—Chapter 6

"Made for You" by One Republic
"Can you feel all the love, like it was made for you?"
"The crowd was wild with joy. These would be the people we lived the closest to, and they were all looking forward to catching the first glimpses of the girls coming to town. One of us would be their queen someday."—Chapter 8

"Fences" by Paramore
"You're always on display for everyone to watch and learn from. Don't you know by now?"
"Sure enough, teams of people with cameras were

wandering around the room, zooming in on girls' shoes, and interviewing them."—Chapter 9

"The Middle" by Jimmy Eat World

"Hey, don't write yourself off yet. It's only in your head you feel left out."

"'I'm not mysterious,' I interrupted.

'You are a little. And sometimes people don't know whether to interpret silence as confidence or fear. They're looking at you like you're a bug so maybe you'll feel like you are one.'"—Chapter 10

"Mercy" by One Republic

"All I wanted to do, is fall apart now."

"'Circumstances being what they are, I haven't had the opportunity to fall in love. Have you?'

'Yes,' I said matter-of-factly."—Chapter 10

"It's a Disaster" by OK Go

"It's a disaster. It's an incredible mess."

"I couldn't even look him in the eye. I didn't know how to explain I had been prepped to expect a dog, that the darkness and privacy made me feel strange, that I'd only ever been alone with one other boy and that was how we behaved."—Chapter 12

"Let the Flames Begin" by Paramore

"This is how we dance when, when they try to take us down."

"It didn't take more than that for me to comprehend. There were rebels inside the grounds."—Chapter 13

"Two Sisters" by Fiction Plane

"Gorgeous eyes, to the right, to the left of me."

"He'd seen at least a dozen girls based on their smiles. We'd spent the better part of the evening together last night, and all he did was make me cry. What kind of friend held those kinds of secrets while making me spill all my own?"—Chapter 16

"A Beautiful Mess" by Jason Mraz

"I like being submerged in your contradictions, dear, 'cause here we are, here we are."

"I didn't expect it, but a warmth filled me.
He'd wanted his first kiss to be with me."—Chapter 18

"The Bones of You" by Elbow

"But I love the bones of you, that I will never escape."

"He was alien and familiar at once. So many of the things around him seemed wrong. But those eyes . . . those were Aspen's eyes."—Chapter 20

"A Little Less Sixteen Candles, A Little More 'Touch Me'" by Fall Out Boy

"I confess, I messed up, dropping 'I'm sorry's like you're still around."

"He stopped in front of my bed and quietly laid the staff he was holding on the ground. 'Do you love him?'

I looked into Aspen's deep eyes, barely visible in the dark.
For a split second, I didn't know what to say.
'No.'"—Chapter 22

"Faint" by Linkin Park
"Don't turn your back on me, I won't be ignored."
"'We're under attack. We have to get you to the base-
ment.'"—Chapter 23

"All At Once" by the Fray
*"There are certain people you just keep coming back to. She is
right in front of you."*
"'If this were a simpler matter, I'd have eliminated everyone
else by now. I know how I feel about you.'"—Chapter 24

"Mexican Standoff" by Elbow
*"Shifting my weight now from foot to foot. What did she see in
this man?"*
"'So you're choosing him over me?' he asked miserably.
'No, I'm not choosing him or you. I'm choosing me.'"
—Chapter 25

"Spinning" by Jack's Mannequin
"I lost my place but I can't stop this story."
"I pulled back the covers and leaped into the morning."
—Chapter 25

THE ELITE:
THE OFFICIAL PLAYLIST

❧·❦

"I WON'T GIVE UP" BY JASON MRAZ

"'Cause even the stars they burn, some even fall to the earth."

"He was graciously giving me time to move on while attempting to find someone else he'd be happy with in the event I couldn't ever love him.

As he moved his head, inhaling just above my hairline, I considered it. What would it be like to simply love Maxon?

'Do you know when the last time was that I really looked at the stars?' he asked."—Chapter 1

"SECRET" BY THE PIERCES

"If I show you, then I know you won't tell what I said."

"'Well, how about this? You can take the book and keep it for a few days.'

'Am I allowed to do that?' I asked in awe.

'No.' He smiled."—Chapter 3

"ANIMAL" BY NEON TREES

"Here we go again. I kinda wanna be more than friends."

"In a split second, I realized that the thought of Maxon

being in love with someone else made me so jealous I couldn't stand it."—Chapter 4

"You Found Me" by Kelly Clarkson

"You broke through, all of my confusion."

"In Aspen's eyes I saw a thousand different endings to that sentence, all of them connecting him to me. That he was still waiting for me. That he knew me better than anyone. That we were the same. That a few months at the palace couldn't erase two years. No matter what, Aspen would always be there for me."
—Chapter 6

"On Fire" by Switchfoot

"I'm standing on the edge of me, I'm standing on the edge."

"For that moment, it felt like we were the only two people in the world."—Chapter 8

"The Pretender" by Foo Fighters

"I'm finished making sense, done pleading ignorance."

"I hopped over the railing, clumsy in my dress and heeled shoes. 'Marlee! Marlee!' I screamed, running as quickly as I could. I almost got to the steps; but two guards caught up with me, and that was a fight I couldn't win."—Chapter 9

"LOVE DOESN'T LAST TOO LONG" BY THE WEEPIES

"And I wish I was wrong, but love doesn't last too long."

"'America, I know you're upset, but please? I told you; you're the only one. Please don't do this.'"—Chapter 10

"HIT ME WITH YOUR BEST SHOT" BY PAT BENATAR

"You don't fight fair, but that's okay, see if I care."

"Celeste looked over her shoulder just in time to see me lunge at her."—Chapter 11

"ENDLESSLY" BY THE CAB

"I'm no angel, I'm just me, but I will love you endlessly."

"'It's just the way it is. The sky is blue, the sun is bright, and Aspen endlessly loves America.'"—Chapter 12

"THE BEST IMITATION OF MYSELF" BY BEN FOLDS

"Maybe I'm thinking myself in a hole, wondering who I am when I ought to know."

"I was excluded, perhaps on purpose, and no one even noticed.

I held it together through the *Report*. I even made it through dismissing my maids. But once I was alone, I broke down."—Chapter 14

"APOCALYPSE PLEASE" BY MUSE

"Declare this an emergency. Come on and spread a sense of urgency."

"But I could feel an urgency tonight. Something might go wrong and this could be our last kiss."—Chapter 15

"Good Time" by Owl City

"Doesn't matter when, it's always a good time then."

"When I raised my glass to our guests, they shrieked with delight, downing their glasses and then throwing them against the walls. Kriss and I weren't expecting that and shrugged before tossing ours as well."—Chapter 19

"Never Say Never" by The Fray

"Picture, you're the queen of everything. As far as the eye can see, under your command."

"That was the question, wasn't it? I still didn't know if I could do the job, but I wasn't sure I wanted to give up on it. And seeing this kindness in Maxon shifted my heart. There was still so much to consider, but I couldn't give up. Not now."—Chapter 20

"They Don't Know About Us" by One Direction

"They don't know what we do best. It's between me and you, our little secret."

"'Maxon doesn't exactly know we're competing, so he might not be able to try as hard. But then, I have to hide, so it's not like I can give you everything he can. It's not really a fair fight either way.'"—Chapter 22

"Believe in What You Want" by Jimmy Eat World

"Your camera flash on us, meaningless."

"I decided I couldn't ask Maxon about the diary yet. He seemed so humble about these things—the way he led, the kind of king he wanted to be—that I couldn't demand answers from him that I wasn't anywhere close to sure he had."—Chapter 24

"Feeling Sorry" by Paramore

"And I'm getting bored waiting 'round for you. We're not getting any younger."

"Maxon shook his head. 'That's not acceptable. I need an answer. Because I can't send someone who really wants this—who really wants me—home if you're going to bail out in the end.'"—Chapter 25

"That's What You Get" by Paramore

"If I ever start to think straight, this heart will start a riot in me."

" 'Are we seriously fighting over some stupid project?'
I turned on him. 'No. We're fighting because you don't get it either.'"—Chapter 26

"Ex-Girlfriend" by No Doubt

"I kinda always knew I'd end up your ex-girlfriend. I hope I hold a special place with the rest of them."

"I kept waiting for him to tell her to get off him, to tell her she wasn't what he wanted. But he didn't. Instead he kissed her."—Chapter 26

"BRICK BY BORING BRICK" BY PARAMORE

"We'll dig a deep hole, to bury the castle."

"I inhaled. 'I think we should eliminate the castes.'"
—Chapter 27

"RULED BY SECRECY" BY MUSE

"Change in the air, and they'll hide everywhere."

"And then, like bees intent on landing, small, quick things
buzzed into the hall. A guard was struck and fell back,
his head hitting the marble with a disturbing crack.
The blood pouring from his chest made me scream."
—Chapter 28

"POISON AND WINE" BY THE CIVIL WARS

"I don't have a choice, but I still choose you."

"It wasn't like I made his world better. It was like I *was* his
world. It wasn't some explosion; it wasn't fireworks.
It was a fire, burning slowly from the inside out."
—Chapter 29

"MERCY" BY DUFFY

"Now you think that I, will be something on the side."

"Kriss was my toughest competition, but she was also the
closest friend I had here."—Chapter 31